The
WHITE ISLE

The WHITE ISLE
by Darrell Schweitzer

illustrated
by Stephen Fabian

Öwlswick Press   Philadelphia

Wildside Press
BERKELEY HEIGHTS • NEW JERSEY

A substantially different version of this novel
was serialized in *Fantastic Stories* April-July 1980
and is © 1980 by Darrell Schweitzer

Published by

Wildside Press
PO Box 45
Gillette, NJ 07933-0045
www.wildsidepress.com

This, my First Novel, is dedicated,
in strict adherence to Tradition,
to my Mother — besides, it's her favorite.

Hear me!

Hear now, O Lords and Ladies, the tale of Evnos and Riacinera, and of the doom of the House of Iankoros.

Hear me!

The Prince

WHAT WERE his first things? His name was Evnos Rae Karavasha, and he was the fifty-seventh Prince of the isle of Iankoros, descended in an unbroken line from the second son of the first king the world ever knew. The sons of the first son had ruled on the Amyrthelian mainland and were called Kings. They had perished long ago. The sons of the second held the island and flourished. They were the Princes.

Evnos was born on a dark October day, in a room hung with red cloth, and his mother died in the birthing. Rannon, the Lord of Death, took her. When the boy was three years old, again in October, Rannon took his father also, and Evnos was Prince over Iankoros. On that day they brought him, shivering and uneasy, out into the drizzling rain, and he stood in the courtyard of the Phoenix Nest, the castle of the Princes, with many men and women around him. Dark clouds drifted overhead. Cloaks and veils flapped in the damp wind.

His father lay on a litter before him, dressed in all his finery and surrounded by costly goods, the best cloth, the rarest jewels, cunningly fashioned swords, a shining helmet, chests of gold coins, and sealed jars of wine. On the other side his honor guard flanked him, stiff and pale as marble statues. Black banners swayed overhead, dripping rainwater.

The Master of Troops came and laid a gift of spices before his departed lord. He spoke aloud:

1

"Rannon, dread king above all kings, you who hold the sword forever over us and who spares each man for a little space of years as it pleases you, we beg you to take these gifts and this man, and by the richness of the offering be moved to mercy. Treat our Prince well when he comes into your kingdom."

The Master of Troops wept. The soldiers looked on in silence.

The boy fidgeted with the gold necklace he wore. He did not understand, and very little of the grief of the others carried over to him. He looked slowly about, counting the pigeons as they huddled under the eaves against the weather. He did not know what this was all about. He did not know what death was.

Why did his father lie so still?

They took up the body on a litter, and for the treasure there were many bearers. At a command, the drawbridge of the Phoenix Nest was lowered. The mourners walked in single file behind their lord: first the guards of honor; then the new Prince accompanied by the wizard and regent Zio Theremderis, who held him by the hand; then the Master of Troops; the lords and ladies of the court; and the soldiers. Common folk joined them as they went, trailing far behind. The procession passed over the bare, brown hills of Iankoros, bowed against the wind and rain and sleet, singing dirges and bearing plain black banners aloft. From afar the mourners looked like a sluggish, weary serpent stretching across the land.

They came to the Black Cliffs. Far below, the sea crashed onto a narrow beach. There waited the old Prince's funeral ship; and the litter, together with all the riches given to Rannon, was lowered with ropes down to waiting sailors. They loaded the corpse and treasure aboard the ship, unfurled a single square sail — black, with the emblem of the Princes of Iankoros, the sign of the Phoenix, embroidered on it in gold — and they launched the vessel out over the breakers, wading out with it until a wind came and took it off to the north, where it vanished after a time in the mist and distance. All present shouted the name of the deceased as loud as they could, and never again did they speak his name. He belonged to Rannon now.

On the march back to the castle, when the child-Prince was sure that the affair was over, when he began to understand that his father was not coming back, he tugged the sleeve of Zio Theremderis and said, "Must it always be like this?"

Months later the sun returned to the castle above the sea, and white flowers, then grass, covered the brown hills, while bees hummed in the orchards and blossoms fell thick as snow.

Throughout that spring and summer the boy Evnos grew. He was

2

a lively child, full of energy and curiosity, always the dismay of his tutors and nurses, who swore he never remained in one place more than an instant.

Zio Theremderis was the center of his world. The wizard towered over him, his long gray beard infinitely mysterious, and it seemed to Evnos that there could be nothing finer to have such a beard, and to practice magic. When Theremderis was not holding court and making the boy sit still with him to receive ambassadors and lords, the wizard dwelt high above everyone else in the Tower of Eagles, so called because of the birds carved in stately procession just beneath its battlements. More than anything else, Evnos wanted to learn what the wizard did up there. One day, he decided to find out.

He slipped away from his attendants, and by luck the guard at the door of the Tower of Eagles was lax, not noticing the boy as he entered. Once inside, the Prince saw a stone staircase winding around inside the tower, up to a distant trapdoor.

He began to climb the well-worn stones, and it seemed to take forever, the door above getting slowly closer. Once he peered down at the steps coiling below him. The floor at the tower's base seemed no larger than a shield.

He drew back, terrified, clinging to the wall of the tower. A spider fell on him in a shower of dirt. He brushed it off in disgust and continued his long climb. Three more times he paused to rest, never looking down. He concentrated on each step as he mounted it. When he finally reached the top, he only knew so because his head hit wooden planking.

Slowly, with every attempt at stealth, he raised the trapdoor and climbed into the room above. He almost lost hold of the door, but caught it again, and lowered it carefully into place without a sound. He saw Zio Theremderis sitting at a desk amid piles of books, with bones and bottles and a stuffed crocodile or two on the shelves around him and a piece of parchment unrolled on the desktop beneath his beard. The old eyes strained to read what was written, and at times Theremderis would lean very low, till his nose all but touched the paper.

"What's that?"

"Magic," Theremderis said without looking up.

"I want to learn magic. I climbed all the way up here to see."

The old man smiled and looked away from the parchment.

"Well! You certainly are a brave boy, and my guard is a fool. Of course I knew he was. That's why I put him there."

"I wasn't afraid. Not very much."

"You have the makings of a hero then. That is good. The world needs heroes. But first you must learn many things."

"Like magic?"

3

"Magic is one of them. Wisdom is another. To rule a kingdom or to wield magic, you must be wise."

"Can we start with magic?"

"I suppose so. What would you like to learn?"

"Magic!"

"Yes, but there are many kinds. What do you want to do first?"

The boy ran to the window. He paid scant attention to the view; he had seen Iankoros many times before from towers almost as high as this one. He took in the other towers and rooftops at a glance, and the walls beyond. Patrolling guardsmen looked like specks. Green hills rolled, spotted with villages, and the blue sea glared beneath the sun. The mainland was barely visible on the horizon, faint, like a motionless cloud.

"Come here," he said, and the wizard came. "See that?" He pointed to a pigeon atop one of the nearer roofs. "I want to make that bird disappear."

Theremderis went back to his desk, took a pen, and wrote something on a scrap of paper.

He gave the boy the paper.

"Say this word. Can you recognize the letters?"

Slowly, clumsily, Evnos sounded out each syllable of the massive word, and uttered it.

In a flash of light, the pigeon vanished.

"There! I did it! I did it! My first magic!"

Theremderis was solemn.

"Yes, the pigeon is gone. I don't suppose anyone will notice, except perhaps its mate. She will sit up day and night, waiting for the bird to return, and he never will. And then there are the baby birds who will starve and die because no one will bring them food anymore."

Horror came to the child's face.

"Bring him back! Quick!"

The wizard shook his head sadly. "I can't. You killed him. You used your magic foolishly, without considering its effect. Perhaps our next lesson should be concerned with wisdom."

Evnos began to cry. He buried his face in the wizard's gown and sobbed for a long time. When he stopped, Theremderis took him in his arms and carried him all the way down to the base of the tower. Neither said a word.

Over the years the Prince grew and there was great promise in him. He was a handsome boy, with a thin, fair face beneath a mass of brown curls, and he had a good disposition and a quick wit. Under the tutelage of Zio Theremderis, his regent, he learned much and learned it quickly, and soon his erudition startled many visitors to the court. He could read and write his own language fluently by the

4

time he was six, and at seven he could speak Sityani. A year later he began to compose good verse in the classical mode. Scholars and foreign dignitaries sat in at his readings, not entirely out of dutiful politeness.

As the Prince entered his teens, new instructors were summoned, military men to teach him the arts of war. They too were pleased with him. Though he was still slender and not very tall, and it was clear he would never be the giant his father had been, he was quick and agile, and patient in discomfort. He wore the heaviest armor without complaint. Soon he was quite skilled with the sword. No one could outrun him. He learned strategy quickly, and soon he was winning battles on paper which had baffled famous heroes on the field. When it came time for war games he was a splendid figure, speaking with a real voice of command. The soldiers loved him.

Then, for the first time since that day in the tower, Theremderis touched on the subject of magic. He amazed the young Prince with elementary feats of illusion. He took him on long flights through the air, over many lands of the world, and more than once transformed him into some beast or fowl, that he might see things through new eyes. Usually, when these transformations were over, the boy would laugh at what he had seen, and the absurdity of mankind would give spice and substance to his verse.

Magic itself, Evnos discovered, when one got down to the mechanics of it, was not all that exciting. First, Theremderis delivered long lectures, for weeks on end, punctuated by strenuous questionings, on the history and philosophy of the Art as expounded by various ancient sages, and Evnos had to memorize the names and deeds (and occasional dooms) of all the master wizards the world had ever known.

Then came the basic techniques. Evnos hoped that he would soon be able to conjure something, but found himself doing more, endlessly more rote-memory work, struggling to learn all manner of formulae and secret words.

"When you're right in the middle of something, you don't have time to look it up," Theremderis kept saying. "And you have to get it *right*. You won't live to be a quarter my age if you don't. The Art is unforgiving. Remember that always."

To make matters worse, most incantations seemed to fall into forms the way classical poetry did, but had no system of *sound* to them. No rhyme, no meter — the ear could not tell when the form was slightly off. Each of the standard incantations had to be memorized completely, syllable by syllable. He had to be able to write them all down with perfect clarity. Even penmanship counted. One letter misformed or left out could change the whole meaning — and effect.

5

Finally they came to deep magic, the summoning of spirits, the divination of the future.

"These things," Theremderis said with the utmost gravity, "are to be used only when all earthly resources have failed. Better it is to pluck a white-hot iron out of the furnace with your bare hands than to call upon a being from the Outer Regions. Summon one only when you have nothing to lose, when all is already lost. Don't even consider doing it otherwise."

He showed Evnos how a certain stone could be removed from the wall of his study. Behind it in a little space was a golden casket which could be opened only with a word. He told the boy the word and bade him speak it. On the third try, the lid came off. Within was the Scroll of Summoning.

Quite unlike many magical documents the Prince had seen, this one was not stained and moldering, nor was it written in some arcane script. It looked like a supply list some steward might make. There were no mystical signs on it, only three columns written in a modern hand, perhaps Theremderis's own. They were the names of all the demons that were known to have names, and the words of binding and unbinding for each.

This was the key to all serious sorcery. The boy handled it gently, looked it over, and put it back in the box. He spoke the opening word backwards and the lid reaffixed itself.

Theremderis put the box back behind the stone.

"I hope you never have to use that," he said.

Evnos hoped so too, and heeded his teacher in all things.

2 "Gone the Eagle, Gone the Dove"

ONE AFTERNOON in the summer of his sixteenth year, Evnos looked out the window of the Tower of Eagles and saw a long column of men coming up from the sea — soldiers whose armor gleamed and flashed in the sun, standard-bearers, serving men with burdens on their backs, courtiers walking beneath canopies, and two great litters, each borne by a dozen porters. Dust rose from beneath their feet as they approached.

The Prince called his teacher to him, saying, "What is this?"

Theremderis answered, "A king comes among us and shall dine within these walls tonight. His daughter is with him, and they say she is a jewel. She is of marriageable age."

"Marriageable age?"

"My Prince, it is time you took a wife."

"I hadn't thought about it. There were so many other things —"

"Don't concern yourself. I have made all the arrangements."

"Teacher, will you always arrange my affairs?"

Theremderis smiled. "Only for a little while yet. Then, perhaps, you shall arrange mine."

Her name was Riacinera, and she was fair and slender. Evnos could hardly make out her face beneath her veils. He thought he saw a flash of a smile.

Her father, the King of the citadel of Sityan Veras and all the

7

lands around it, was a broad-shouldered, muscular man, a little gone over to fat. His face was overly powdered, his gray beard dripping with perfume. The clothing he wore was so intricate and garish to the Prince's eye that nothing stood out against the rest.

The King gave his greeting without a bow or a nod, standing before the Iankorosian throne: "Hail, illustrious Prince who shall live long and rule well. May the friendship of our realms be as firm as the great oaks which grow in my country."

Evnos glanced up at Theremderis, who stood by his side, then sat back against the carven throne.

"And may your land ever be rich," he said, "and may the rains continue to fall and the oaks grow as tall as the mountains. May those mountains hold back your enemies forever."

"Behold," said the King. "I have brought you many gifts." He clapped his hands and men came forward bearing fine jewelry and swords, folds of the best silks, and the polished horn of the *glimmich*, which was straight and thin and as long as a cavalry lance.

"I have gifts for you," said the Prince, presenting his guest with jars of spices brought from afar by ships of Iankoros; bottles of the best wine, for which the isle was famous; gold ornaments; a necklace made from the teeth of the mantichore; and a magic stone which always knew the directions.

They feasted in the largest dining hall of the Phoenix Nest, and all were impressed by the courtesy of the Prince, who always knew what to say and do, when to lead and when to follow. Theremderis stood near him always, unobtrusive, communicating much with a glance, a nod, a gesture.

At table the Prince sat beneath a huge shield blazoned with the emblem of his house. The King of Sityan Veras sat on his right, Zio Theremderis on his left. Riacinera, the King's daughter, was fifteen years of age, Evnos learned. She sat with her women at the other end, still mysterious behind her veils. Fifty great lords and ladies sat between the intended couple on either side of the table. Not once during the meal did the two exchange any words other than formal greeting, although Evnos gazed upon her and she upon him, each looking away quickly if they thought anyone had noticed.

Theremderis and the King both secretly smiled.

For hours dancers danced and musicians played. Poets recited passages from *The Song of the Great Stone*, which was a long, vivid, gloomy epic of unimaginable antiquity. Evnos wondered why it was being performed just then, but some of the lines stayed with him:

In the middle of light there is shadow.
In the middle of shadow there is darkness.
In the middle of darkness there is Rannon.

8

They were like a sudden, chill breeze on a summer's day. He never forgot them.

When the *Song* was done, there came the *Hitarmaal*, a tale of the Laughing Hero, who married the most beautiful woman in the world at the end. This seemed more appropriate.

All the while the feasters sampled more delicacies than could be catalogued by anyone other than the master cook. Lamp smoke and incense swirled beneath the ceiling while speech and music filled the hall. Toasts were proposed and drunk and polite courtesies were exchanged, but very little was actually said as the banquet went on and on.

Finally, when the twelfth course (swan's eggs, boiled in honey) had been served and many were sighing, patting stomachs, and loosening belt buckles, all was done and the tables were cleared. Most of the lower ranking guests were dismissed, and couches were brought for everyone else. Evnos, Theremderis, the King, Riacinera and her nurse, and a few favorites reclined in a circle, and a game of Rounds began.

The Prince knew the game almost as second nature and had practiced it many times with Theremderis, who insisted that any courtier, let alone a prince, must prove himself at the ancient poetic sport of Iankoros.

So the game went on around the circle, each player composing a stanza of verse, one after another, until a long ("And usually somewhat disjointed," the wizard used to say) poem was formed. Classical allusions fell thick as sleet. Just outside the circle, secretaries scribbled furiously to get it all down on paper.

There was a cubbyhole somewhere, Evnos knew, stuffed with the dusty effusions of princely Rounds, added to each time whether the game was played well or badly.

This time the game was played well. Evnos stood out above all, and Theremderis too showed great wit, as did the King. His daughter exhibited marvelous fancy. The game had gone on for a while when the wizard leaned over and whispered into the Prince's ear, "Is she not a wonder?"

"Yes. She is."

Then Theremderis's turn came and he delivered a verse, after which Evnos gave one, as did the King, and the poem went around again.

"My Prince," whispered Theremderis, "it would be well if you were to compose a verse complimenting the lady Riacinera. Be subtle, but make yourself understood to those who should understand."

The next time his turn came, Prince Evnos paused, and haltingly at first, then more smoothly, spoke a verse:

9

"Empty perches high above,
Gone the eagle, gone the dove.
Together they are bound in love —
They've flown the whole world over."

He said this while looking into Riacinera's still-veiled face. She smiled shyly and turned away.

The King of Sityan Veras remained for a month in the castle called the Phoenix Nest. There were feasts nearly every evening, and hunts most days; and discussions: readings from famous books and from new ones; plus many more games of Rounds in the evenings.

The Prince saw Riacinera more often. At first he exchanged polite notes with her by messenger, and then carefully supervised visits were arranged, and, after a time, more private ones. When he first saw her without her veil, it struck him how beautiful she was and how pale, and how she seemed to be just a little bit afraid of him just then. He didn't know what to say, and there followed a long, awkward silence. Fortunately Theremderis was present, and he broke that silence, and the difficult moment passed.

Evnos found himself thinking of his bride-to-be at odd times throughout the day, and he would pause in his lessons or his duties to consider the look in her eyes, the way she smiled, the things she had said during their last encounter. In the margins of his notebooks he composed verses to her beauty, while Zio Theremderis looked on and pretended not to notice.

It was a new experience for both the Prince and Princess. Brought up in the isolation of royal courts in the company of scholars and ministers, they had at times developed fondness for certain people, even devotion, but never love. Evnos thought he loved Theremderis in a way, but it was not the same. This new kind of love grew until one day a jittery and stammering Prince of Iankoros, for once not the least bit eloquent, blurted the whole matter out to his teacher as they sat over a book.

The wizard smiled and stroked his beard, as if deep in thought.

When the wedding was held, and Evnos and Riacinera left the great hall hand-in-hand, dressed in matching, diamond-studded gowns, they went into a secret chamber. The door closed behind them. The Prince heard a guard take his place outside, pike thumping once against the floor. He knew that this time there would be no interruptions, no supervision. He and his bride were truly alone.

And again he was afraid. He didn't know what to say. He realized that Riacinera was staring at him, eyes wide, almost in terror, as if now, for the first time, she really believed that all this was happening. He realized how little he actually knew her, how little he knew himself, how their lives were filled with mystery.

He tried to laugh. "Uh, we've . . . come to a point, I think . . . I mean . . . Theremderis didn't say anything about . . ."

She laughed, genuinely. "My nurse wasn't much help either."

Suddenly they weren't afraid anymore. They sat together in silence for a while, and he reflected on how Theremderis had manipulated him, brought him to this strange moment. But now he accepted everything. He was glad that his life had turned out this way. The marriage was, of course, arranged. Neither of them were ready for it. But he was discovering that he actually loved Riacinera. He desperately hoped that she felt the same about him.

When much of the night had passed, they were boy and girl no longer. Toward the dawn, they got up and peered out through a window. The stars shone clearly in the dark sky. The Moon was long past full, only recently risen. A pair of pigeons sat together on a nearby rooftop, barely visible in the dim light.

The east began to glow. Evnos saw, just before the stars faded, that the Sun would rise in the House of the Dragon, near the field of the Phoenix.

These were good signs.

A year passed and Theremderis rested, his long labor completed. Evnos Rae Karavasha, now Prince of Iankoros in the fullness of the title, ruled well. He studied the reports of his ministers and gave instructions. He walked over the island with an entourage of officials and clerks, learning more than he had ever known about how the people lived, how they felt. He talked to them, trying to treat them, if not as equals, then as valued and respected subjects.

At times Evnos came to Theremderis still, but there was little left to teach. In formal court, the wizard stood farther behind the throne than before. He did not have to nod; they did not exchange glances. The young man knew what to do.

It seemed that everyone loved the Prince and his new Lady. There were few intrigues. When rivals quarreled, Evnos would enjoin them to forgive offenses, to be reconciled, and he was always obeyed. He had a kind of persuasive innocence, it seemed. This, the wizard reflected, might be more valuable than wisdom.

Riacinera was like that too. Theremderis still had only an impression of her: very intelligent, reserved, a child and a woman at the same time. He wondered if Evnos had any true understanding of her mysteries.

The castle was always decked out in celebration. If the wizard had

11

any worry, it was that his former pupil was more interested in pleasing his bride than in running the kingdom. Or so it seemed. There were so many grand balls, dances, fêtes, hunts. The old man found the pace tiring. He excused himself from as many of them as he could.

But in time his worry diminished. In her subtle way, Lady Riacinera was more practical-minded than her husband. She steered him back when he drifted from more important business.

It was a more perfect match than even he had anticipated.

At the end of the year, not three days into the next, a ship arrived in the harbor of Iankoros bearing messengers from the King of Sityan Veras, Riacinera's father. War had broken out on the mainland. The King bade his ally, the Prince, to bring his armies to him at once. Together they would fight the renegade Count of Baracenese, who had sold himself to the Witch King from beyond the Thousand Hills. The elaboration of the messengers' tale was one of invasions, massacres, and the burning of towns.

Theremderis stood beside Evnos as the news was related.

"So far your reign has been easy," he said. "There have been no challenges. Now you are to be truly tested. Therefore I have one final lesson for you, and a gift."

"Give them, then."

The wizard called for a certain casket to be brought. It was thin, about as long as a man's leg, and plated with beaten brass. Theremderis spoke a word and the lid rose of its own accord, revealing folds of purple cloth. He took out a splendid sword, inlaid with precious stones on the hilt and scabbard. Kneeling down before his former pupil, he proffered the weapon.

"This is Dran. It has been in the family for a long time. Your forefathers wielded it, all of them, back to the first Prince. There is much power in this weapon."

Evnos took the sword out of its scabbard and examined the blade. It was of unexcelled workmanship and the finest metal, with a cool blue sheen to it. Strange signs were carved near the tip. He hefted the sword and found it balanced.

He smiled. "This is a splendid weapon indeed. I shall win glory with it. You will be proud of me."

"And now for the lesson," said Theremderis with a sigh.

"The lesson? Oh, yes."

"Do you remember when you were a child and you made a pigeon disappear?"

"I remember."

"This sword is like that word you spoke. Don't draw it unless you mean to use it."

"In this war I certainly mean to use it!"

12

"Beware of rashness, my Prince. The story goes that the Dwarf king who wrought this blade, out of the perversity of his nature, placed a doom upon it, and that doom was, 'Many heads shall this sword cut off, but the last shall be the head of wisdom.' These things are always more complicated than they seem. I interpret this doom to mean that the last of your line shall use this sword rashly and destroy himself and his house. Be careful."

The Prince turned the blade over in his hands, examining it closely. Then he sheathed it again.

"Do you believe . . . the story?"

Theremderis shrugged. "I don't know. But the lesson is worthwhile."

"Yes, of course. But all my ancestors have avoided this doom, so it can't be that difficult. Nevertheless, I shall be careful, and only cut off the heads of my enemies."

"May you win fame."

Then Evnos swore a mighty oath on the blade, with Zio Theremderis as witness, that he would fight this war for the honor of his house, for the continued glory of Iankoros, and to fulfill his obligation to his ally. He would make Iankoros envied among nations and bring home the richest spoils.

By his life, his honor, his land, his ancient lineage and the sword Dran he swore.

The war was fast and furious. There were forced marches, camps set up in precarious positions, armies hurried over mountains. Desperate battles echoed along narrow passes, through the thick forests, up and down rocky slopes. And all the while the Prince was true to his oath.

He had never seen anything like this war. At times he was terrified, but he did not show it. At times he gloried in his own deeds and those of others. At times it seemed like a sharp, strange dream, something from which he would awake in Iankoros amazed.

Terrible spells were cast and turned away by sorcerers in both armies, and the night skies flickered with the power of the castings. Swords sang on shields. Arrows flew like swarms of bees. In the end, the Prince led the small force that swung around behind the treacherous Count and scattered his troops. Victory came within days. The armies gathered before Baracenese, finding the citadel hastily and poorly prepared for a siege. By intrigue, it was arranged for a sally-port to be left open. In the middle of the night, Evnos led the attack. The guards died quietly. When his men opened the main gate, it was he who stood on the wall and blew the trumpet to signal the final assault.

That morning, the Count's head hung from his own gate.

The Prince's name was carried far and wide by herald and by minstrel, and his own people rejoiced in his deeds. But the Evnos who finished the war was not the same who had begun it. He was no longer the frail youth who followed his teacher around the court of Iankoros carrying books. Now he was broader across the shoulders, well-muscled, his face bronzed by the sun. When he stood in his armor, it seemed he had been wearing it for a long time.

Eight months had passed since he left home. The victors quarreled over spoils, but inevitable reconciliations followed, then feasts, games, and endless drinkings of toasts. Evnos tried to stay aloof when the allies squabbled. His father-in-law, the King, was constantly called on to settle matters.

Then a messenger came from Iankoros. He stood, sweaty, breathless before the Prince in his tent.

"What news?"

"My Prince, I came as fast as I could. I rode two horses nearly to death, I —"

"What *news?*"

A broad smile spread over the messenger's face.

"My Lord, it is your lady. She is near to her time. Your child is about to be born!"

Evnos bolted to his feet. At once he was shouting orders to his men. They were to depart. Leaving behind a captain to represent him and to haggle over the loot, he took leave of the King and went directly to his ship.

Swiftly the oarsmen carried him down the river Arrax. The sail caught a strong wind just beyond the delta, and the ship slid past Nedek, the great port town, without stopping. Already Iankoros was on the horizon, like the hump of a whale rising out of the sea. Evnos stood on the deck, urging his crewmen on, speaking spells to call up a better wind. The oarsmen strained at their benches, but they understood. No one complained.

A son! He hoped it would be a son. He prayed to the distant gods, the gods who had withdrawn far from Earth, and to the lesser deities who had remained, and to the spirits, that it would be a boy. A son and heir to continue his line. The thought of a fifty-eighth prince made him want to whoop for joy. All the gold he had won in the war meant very little just then.

He thought of Riacinera and hoped she wasn't in too much pain. Her time would come . . . soon, and then he hoped to see her sitting up in bed, smiling, cradling her son in her arms.

Hours passed. The island loomed huge before them, the ship dwarfed by great cliffs as the mariners worked their way around, through reefs and treacherous currents, until they came to the narrow passage that led to the harbor. Already the Prince could almost

14

feel every step of the way up from the docks and along the roads. He could hear the drawbridge groaning down to admit him. He imagined the familiar courtyards, which he had last looked upon in another season. But he knew he would not tarry there. He would run the rest of the way, up the stairs, into the bedchamber.

The sun sank in a splash of glory, and the starry-eyed night looked down. The towering mass of the island turned slowly, breakers foaming at the base of the cliffs. Finally there was an opening in the stern, unscalable face of Iankoros. The vessel slid gingerly into the narrow channel, the sail limp, oars scraping stone on either side. Then the ship reached the still waters beyond. When the guardsmen recognized the Prince's ship, they cheered and waved torches from their watchtowers.

Evnos could not wait any longer. He stripped off his armor and weapons, laid aside his outer garments, and before the astonished eyes of his crew leapt into the cold waters of the lagoon and swam to the nearest dock. Eager hands helped him up out of the water. Startled faces gaped. When the sailors from his own ship saw him there they cheered, then moored the vessel at their leisure.

"I am coming!" he shouted into the night. Clad only in his light underclothes, shoeless, he ran with long strides through winding streets, where shops and storehouses leaned against the castle walls. He came to the Phoenix Nest. At first the sentry challenged this half-naked and dripping fellow who came in out of the darkness, but when he saw the Prince's face, he stood aside. Evnos padded over the drawbridge, over the flagstones of the courtyard within; then he came to a hallway and his feet were silent on thick carpets. He bounded up the stairway of the main hall, taking three steps at a time until finally, out of breath, he stood before the golden doors of Lady Riacinera's chamber.

And there, shocking against the gold, were three women dressed in black, weeping. A soldier stood at attention, black ribbons draped around his spear.

Evnos was completely bewildered. He was suddenly empty inside, unable to say or do anything. He merely gaped, swaying as he stood, breathing hard.

"What does this mean?" he finally managed to ask. "Why do you weep? Why aren't you . . . celebrating?"

Then one of the women, one whose face he recognized through her veil, spoke.

"She is dead. Alas, she is dead."

"*Who* is dead? What are you talking about?"

But he already knew. The realization was like a battle wound. At first there was only the numbing blow. . . . The pain would come later.

15

Again the woman said, "She is dead. O my Lord! The Lady Ria-cinera is dead!" She broke down, sobbing.

He looked from one veiled face to the next, to the next, and still he stood like one dreaming. He was waiting for one of them to say it wasn't so.

. . . And then the pain came.

"No! No! No!" he screamed. He fell to his knees and pounded on the floor with his fists, shrieking in short, hysterical bursts. "No! She is not dead! She is not!"

"She is," said one of the women softly. The guard holding the spear turned away, hiding his face.

The Prince leapt up and heaved the doors open.

"Beloved! Speak to me! I am here!"

The bed was empty. A wreath of drooping flowers hung from one of the bedposts. He stood there for a moment, then leaned against the doorway, limp, and slid back to the floor.

"And the child?" he asked in a low voice.

Two of the women wailed. The eldest one, who had spoken first, found the strength to speak again.

"Never born."

"And Riacinera? Where *is* she?"

"We could not leave her until you returned. Surely Rannon would have been angry if denied his due, and would send us a curse. This morning the wizard Theremderis came to this room with many men. They took your Lady to the Black Cliffs. They put her in a fine ship and filled it with treasure to buy favor for her from the boar-headed one. My Prince, she is in the Underearth now!"

The woman could say no more. She shrank away from him.

Rannon, god of death — he had Riacinera now. What was he doing with her? What? Was he touching her now?

Evnos went to his own chamber, dressed, and left the castle by a secret tunnel. He ran the length of the island, to the Black Cliffs. There was nothing he could hope to see, only the empty, endless ocean, the bare shore, the stars and the waves. He remembered this place from his childhood. He had always avoided it, as if by instinct. Now he understood why.

The sheer granite face of the cliff dropped down into shadows, luminous foam washing the feet of the stones.

He gazed to the north, that most evil of directions, where lay the realm of Rannon, and he cried out in a loud voice:

"Rannon! Pig! Hear me! You shall not have her! I curse your name! *You shall not have her!*"

A hand touched him on the shoulder. He whirled. Zio Theremderis

16

stood there. He had not seen his teacher in months, but now the sight was not welcome.

"*You.*"

"It is I. Calm yourself."

"How can I calm myself after what you have done?"

Theremderis was expressionless. "My Prince," he said in a low voice. "What have I done?"

"*You gave her up!* You gave her to Rannon."

"Lord, she was dead. There was nothing else to do."

"*Nothing?*"

"My Lord, a plague came to this island. I saw the spirit of it in the sky, sowing death from between its fingers. The pestilence was in the air, on the wind, in the sea, everywhere. It fell with each rain. It lingered in the dew. Many died. I, naturally, took every precaution for your lady's safety. Her food was cleansed. I used every spell to seal her chambers, but still the sickness reached her. I wrestled with Rannon, using all my art, but he won, as he always wins in the end. Leechcraft, the lore of books, my spells, healing stones — all were useless. She died in a delirium, calling your name. I beg you, mourn her now as is fitting, but do not rage against what is inevitable. Come away now."

He put his hand on the Prince's arm, but Evnos shook it off.

"I will *not* come away!"

"The humours of the night will make you ill."

Despite the chill, the Prince was streaming with perspiration.

"No. I have to figure out what I'll do. I'll plan my campaign against Rannon. I'm successful in war now, so tell me what you know of my enemy. What ships does Rannon have? How many soldiers? How many horse? Where might his fortifications be breached? *Tell me!*"

"This is mad talk, Lord. No man knows these things. I don't. No one ever goes into the lands of Rannon and returns to tell about it."

"If you don't know, then I'll find someone who *does!*"

He ran off, back toward the castle. The aging wizard could not keep up with him.

"Wait!"

The voice of Zio Theremderis was lost in the night.

3
Eunos Conjures a Spirit in the Tower of Eagles

THE PRINCE'S HEART was racing as he bounded up the winding stairs of the Tower of Eagles. Quickly he reached the top, climbed through the trapdoor, locked it, and dragged a trunk on top of it. Then he whispered the secret name of fire, and the torches on the walls flamed.

He concentrated on what he was doing, and calmed himself with his deliberation. He shoved tables and chairs aside, piled books in corners, stacked bottles and flasks, clearing a wide, empty space in the middle of the room.

Then he opened a cabinet and took out several bottles. He began his work. With the ashes of the mage Hinaris, the only one of all the ancients to escape the Lord of Death, he made a paste, and with it drew a circle five cubits in diameter on the smooth stones. All the while he spoke invocations to the name of Hinaris, calling on the memory of the Fortunate One to inspire him.

Within the circle he drew a four-pointed star, aligned with the cardinal directions, the northern point blunted. Using ordinary chalk, he wrote the names of his fifty-six predecessors around the outside of the star, the names of sorcerer-princes of Iankoros, going back to Manaris-Zin and the beginning of the world. He spoke each name aloud. This was mostly a formality, for all of them were now the slaves of Rannon, and could not help him.

He drew a triangle inside the star, again with the ash paste, and

18

at the points of the triangle he wrote the three virtues of a wizard: courage, knowledge, and good will. Finally, inside the circle, he drew a square, with the ash again, and wrote his own name in it.

All this completed, he stepped over what he had drawn, careful not to smear any part of it, and put the nearly empty ash-bottle back on the shelf. He took the Scroll of Summoning from behind the loose stone, and with it under one arm he returned to the open cabinet, took out incense burners and placed them around the circumference of the circle. No ordinary powder burned in them this night: in the first, dragon's blood, dried for centuries; in the second, the sweat of the basilisk; in the third, herbs from caves beneath the sea; in the fourth, the ears of a shadow; in the fifth, a stone tongue hacked from the terrible image that Manaris-Zin once carved and no man has beheld since, which stares into the abyss beyond the world's edge; in the sixth, the pulverized claws of a tiger that once spoke; in the seventh, the beard of a sage.

He was ready. The windows were all bolted save one, which opened to the north. He returned to the center of his drawings, stood in the square with his own name beneath his feet, spread the scroll out on the floor, and began his incantations. Each one he had practiced or at least seen Theremderis perform. But the correct recitation of all of them, in the proper order, was something he had never witnessed, let alone performed. He concentrated, speaking each word slowly, carefully.

Smoke rose slowly from the burners, and the room filled with a musty haze. The torches seemed to dim a little. His voice droned on, going down the list of the named spirits and speaking their binding words. He was fishing for those spirits like a man with a hook and line, hoping one would chance to be passing near enough to the Earth to be caught.

Suddenly he felt a chill and a faint tugging in his mind. *He had one.* He glanced back down at the list. The last name he had spoken was *Gladziri,* an ancient and powerful spirit, the bane of King Kalvad of old, and of many less notable sorcerers. Evnos knew that it was too late for any hesitation or doubt. He had to complete what he had begun.

Confidently, then, he raised his arms and summoned Gladziri with the spell of the sheath, the spell of the anchor, and the spell of the driven stake. He felt the freezing cold of the outer abyss, as if he had reached deep into some impossible ice water, far colder than anything in the human world.

The pain was like burning.

And Gladziri came. At first the room was still, and then there was a noise like rustling leaves. A draft blew and torches flickered. The draft rose into a roaring blast. Evnos's hair streamed. He bent low beneath the force of the wind, feeling the presence of the demon as only a sorcerer can. It groped at him from all sides, hate-filled, furious. But the ashes of Hinaris were a wall against it.

And Gladziri spoke, invisible among the cavorting shadows.

"Maggot, who is about to die, you have me here. What do you want?"

"I am not a maggot, but a man," said Evnos. "I am your master now."

"If it pleases you to think so, maggot, then delude yourself all the more. You are merely an inexperienced, incompetent wizardling. Wiser ones know better than to argue in those few seconds I grant them before I split their skulls. You are a maggot like all your kind, a worm that crawls on the dead flesh of this Earth, unable to move among the stars like the higher beings. Are you not afraid of me, little worm?"

"I am not afraid," said Evnos.

"Then *be* afraid!"

The tower burst into flame. Books exploded from the shelves, trailing sparks. Thick, black smoke filled the air, leaving the Prince gasping for breath while his whole body ran with sweat from the furnace-heat. Then the flames raced across the floor as if oil had been spilled there, across the lines of chalk and ash, and fire swirled around his legs.

Yet his clothing did not burn, and there was no pain. He knew now, as he had suspected, as he had steeled his mind to believe, that the flames were mere illusion. The demon withdrew them. The room was as it had been.

There was a snarling outside the tower, followed by shouts and screams. Something came scraping up the sheer stones. The walls shook. Books and bottles tumbled from shelves again. The open window filled for just an instant, then squirming, blood-red shapes poured through, all teeth and claws and lashing tails, spreading across the floor like living jelly. Evnos thought: he could run for the trapdoor, heave the trunk aside and be down the stairs. The things were slow. He could escape those awful mouths —

Which was exactly what Gladziri wanted him to do. When one of the creatures came close enough, he kicked it, and his boot passed through without meeting any resistance. He stayed where he was. He knew that if he left the circle he would be smeared over the walls, and no piece of him bigger than the joint of a finger would ever be found. Such things had happened many times before, to magicians who panicked. But if he remained in the square, the demon could *not* touch him.

All the men he had slain in the war rose against him, their wounds gaping. They cried for vengeance. He made no response, and they vanished.

"Enough!" He spoke the word of Gladziri's binding once more.

"You are better at your art than I first thought, little wizardling. Far better than that one who had me three nights ago. His fate . . . amused me."

Laughter echoed throughout the tower.

"Hear me!" cried the Prince.

"I hear you. Speak your purpose. It grows late."

"I wish to know of Rannon, the Lord of Death."

"*Him?* Why do you wish to know about him? He is a mad fool. You need know nothing more."

"You will explain."

"Every time I have my will of a wizard, Rannon comes to collect the refuse. He alone of the Great Gods still dallies on this miserable little world, playing with worms. It is because his mind is weak. The others have moved on to more mature pastimes."

"Explain further. I command you. Did not the gods die to redeem mankind, for a short while at least, from the clutches of Rannon, as is told in *The Song of the Great Stone?*"

"I care not for your songs and your squealings, little one. And we who feel the heartbeat of the universe do not read your books. Is it not said that only a blind man or a cripple needs a cane? Therefore, you who are blind and crippled and deformed and devoid of wit and manhood, listen to one wiser than yourself for once and learn that *the gods did not die.* They came to their senses. They ceased playing with worms. They do not concern themselves with mankind at all anymore, except for the idiot-god Rannon, who finds his delight in your pain."

"Speak not with such contempt. I have power over you."

"Speak not with such vacuous vanity. You are a nuisance and nothing more."

Evnos caught himself. He was arguing again, and at the end of such arguments Gladziri had doubtless laid a subtle trap. The demon was playing on his pride, now that his fear had proven of no use.

He spoke firmly, remembering his purpose.

"Answer me directly, Gladziri. How may one enter the kingdom of Rannon?"

"I was summoned to tell you *that?* Oh carrion, just step out of that square and I shall send you swiftly into the kingdom of Rannon, to the very place he had prepared for you! All you have to do is *die!* It's very simple. Now dismiss me if you are through with your jabbering."

"I'm not through."

"What then?"

"You have not answered my question."

"I have, unless it was poorly phrased. I will assume, then, that you want to enter the land of the dead while yet living. Is that your grand design? Do you intend to plague the degenerate Rannon? Even he does not deserve you, maggot wizardling. Even he —"

"*Tell me.*"

"The wind and sea are servants to Rannon. Your little gods, who are scarcely more than you are, may send you a breeze occasionally, but Rannon is the master of the hurricane. It is his dog, and he sends it out to fetch ships and sailors for his hoard. Am I going too fast for you? These are complex matters, perhaps more than your dust-and-clay mind can comprehend. To the north of the world, beyond the ice wall, there is a cliff which marks the edge of the domain of Rannon. In the cliff there is an opening which may only be reached by sea. All funeral ships pass through it, bringing new toys to the idiot god. And to his son. Yes, Rannon has a son now, even more a travesty than he is. This creature is called Kanatekelei, and he has no mind at all. The two of you should get along quite well."

"*Tell more.*"

"There are no good places, no pleasant places in the Underearth. Human maggots flatter themselves into thinking that the virtuous are rewarded and the wicked punished. No, they are *all* punished, for the crime of existence. Rannon cares not for the baubles you send him. He takes no bribes. There is no escape from him. Even those whose bodies are destroyed, as in fire, go into the Underearth, into the lands of Rannon. Rannon builds new bodies to house their spirits; and when he is done, they wish they still had the old. Drowned men come to Rannon, too. On the road beneath the world's oceans rides a black coach without coachmen. You can see its lamp below the water on dark nights, if you look. It is gathering up the dead. But don't lean too far to have a look. You might fall in and it will gather you too! Ha!"

"*Tell me*, is it possible to enter Rannon's country undetected?"

"If you are brave enough and clever enough. But you, little maggot, only think you are."

"How could I rescue one from that land? How could I bring her back?"

"You could carry her."

"Leave me," said the Prince. "I am satisfied."

Evnos was triumphant. He had proven himself a mighty wizard by this conjuring. He had gained knowledge no human being had ever held before. Much of it might be terrible, but he did not care. He had learned that one essential thing: *it was possible to get Riacinera back.*

He leapt for joy and clapped his heels together in the air.

22

And at that very instant, a sudden gust blew, and the Scroll of Summoning sailed across the room.

Horror replaced joy. The demon was still present.

"You forgot to say the word of unbinding, wizardling maggot. . . . I am still here. But no matter. Just go over there and pick up the scroll and read the word. *What can be the problem?*"

Evnos lifted one foot, then froze. He was trapped and he knew it. There would be no defense if he stepped outside of the square.

"A mere formality," crooned Gladziri. "Send me away. Do it."

He shouted every word of unbinding he could think of.

"Alas, that is the wrong one."

The scroll rose in the air, and for an instant Evnos could see long, thin, hideously white fingers holding it, and then it was torn into tiny pieces and scattered in the air.

The torches went out, and Gladziri raged around the room in a whirl of wind and smoke, roaring with laughter. Tables and cabinets splintered. Shelves tore themselves from walls. Bottles and flasks fell like shattering hail. The demon swirled dust and debris and wore them like a cloak. He hurled the incense burners at the hapless conjurer one by one. The tower shook with his mirth. Other things flew, until a steady bombardment of missiles poured into the center of the room. Gladziri could not cross the line of ash paste, but a stone could; a book could; a bench could.

Evnos had nothing to shield himself with, and projectiles struck him out of the blind dark. He couldn't hope to dodge, lest he leave the one safe spot and be torn to pieces.

Gladziri did not need a light to aim by.

Something cracked the Prince on the head and he fell to the floor, vaguely aware of warm blood on his face. He huddled in the middle of the floor, his head tucked down, his arms around his knees. Gladziri tore the loose stone out of the wall and hurled it, and he loosened more. One smashed a shoulder, another a knee.

In a final effort to keep hold on consciousness and mind, Evnos began to recite lines from *The Song of the Great Stone*, but even as he did he saw for the first time the falseness in the account of the deeds of those gods and heroes. The *Song* was nothing more than comforting lies. The universe was not like that, the Prince knew. The gods did not protect men. They had abandoned them, and there was no hope except hope in what men could accomplish alone.

He expected to die soon. He almost wanted to, to get the suffering over with, to rejoin Riacinera. He did not die. Finally there were no more missiles. He lay still, listening to his blood drip.

The torches came back on. A kindly voice said, "All is well. Come out of the square now."

He rolled his head to one side. Only one eye had any sight in it.

Through the haze he made out Zio Theremderis standing just beyond the curving line of ash paste where the outer circle touched one of the star-points.

"Come to me," said the wizard. "I have banished the demon. Let us leave this wretched place."

"Teacher! Help me! I can't move!"

Theremderis only said again, "Come to me."

Then the Prince sobbed in despair, for he understood that this was not Theremderis at all, but Gladziri, torturing him with hope.

The torches extinguished themselves and a piece of nail-studded board slammed into his face, ripping open a cheek. He knew little more. The spirit did not seem to understand that he neared unconsciousness. Perhaps it did not fully understand what it meant to have flesh. Still it persisted with its screams and yells, its foul stenches, threats, missiles, curses, and an endless array of revolting apparitions.

At last dawn came, and the sunlight banished Gladziri as no spell could. Evnos felt someone touch him gently. He stirred into semi-delirium, babbling lines from *The Song of the Great Stone*. When he could see a little bit, he made out the face of Theremderis hovering over him, the true Theremderis, who had crossed the ash line.

"Teacher?"

Theremderis surveyed the ruins around him.

"This was a mighty conjuring."

"I had Gladziri."

"And he had you. You could not dismiss him. Consider yourself fortunate that you still breathe! I could not help you at all last night. I could not enter and face Gladziri unprotected. Even now I shall have to exorcise his influence from this room, lest he return every night and haunt it till the end of time."

The Prince heard nothing more. He tried to say the name of Ria-cinera as the wizard carried him away.

4 A Year in Bed

PRINCE EVNOS SPENT most of his nineteenth year in bed. At first, when his life hung like spider's silk before stormy winds, only the aged wizard tended him. First, his body had to be healed. With spells and leechcraft and splints Theremderis tended him, with rare medicines, with patience and forgiveness and hope. The wizard labored long hours, letting no one else near the young man. And from the doorway of the room in which the Prince lay, he ruled the island again as Regent, listening to the reports of ministers, signing documents, giving instructions.

This was only the beginning of his task. Mending broken bones was the easiest part. The Prince's soul had been burnt by exposure to the spirit, for a spirit is of colors no eye can see, of substance no hand may touch, and of more dimensions than three. From it all that is mortal must recoil as from a raging fire. Experienced wizards are aware of this danger, dismissing spirits as quickly as they can.

Theremderis shook his head sadly. The Prince was, of course, not experienced. Like most young men, he didn't really believe that all the precautions he had learned really applied to him. The catastrophes always happened to someone else, usually someone old.

Carefully, Theremderis drew the poison out. He took his Lord, the Prince who was still his student, to a spacious chamber overlooking the southern sea, and he blessed the room and called fair humours into it. Still the Prince's recovery was a slow, uncertain thing. For

25

weeks he lay in a delirium, screaming strange names and words. Like a rare and delicate glasswork smashed by a hammer, his body and soul lay in ruin. Theremderis had one great fear — that Evnos's mind would never be whole, that he would come out of the ordeal mad — but Theremderis tirelessly reconstructed all that his pupil had been, using secrets only he knew. There was no hurrying nature in the mending of bones. He might speak the true names of these bones and gain power over them, commanding them to grow strong and straight once more, but the slowness of the growth and the sharp flashes of pain that came whenever the patient moved were not something he could control.

All Iankoros knew that some peril had befallen the Prince. People waited, staring up at the castle. They gossiped on street corners and in taverns. Yet no word came. Everyone had seen the lights in the tower on the night of the conjuring. They had heard the explosions, the superhuman shouts; and yet, to hear it from all those attached to the court, nothing extraordinary had happened: everything was officially denied. Soon it was whispered in the streets that the Prince was dead, or perhaps insane, or marvelously and hideously transformed by his sorceries so that the lower half of his body was that of a beast.

There was mourning in every house, not solely because the folk loved their Prince, but because they defined themselves in terms of him. He was their anchor in the sea of history. They were subjects of the descendant of the second son of the first king the world had ever known, whose line was unbroken and pure. For their Prince to be dead or mad or without the possibility of an heir meant that they no longer knew who they were.

One day Evnos sat up in bed and called for Zio Theremderis. He was pale and wasted, his skin stretched tight over his bony chest, his eyes sunken and not quite focussed. There was an ugly scar down the side of his face.

For once, Theremderis was not immediately at hand. The Prince called for a servant and sent for the wizard, his first command in many months. The wizard came. At once a herald was sent into the towns, saying, "The Prince is well." Bells rang. Cooks banged on pots. Housewives danced in the streets. The noise of the celebration came even to Evnos's chamber.

"What's all the commotion?" he asked weakly.

Later, when Evnos was able to remain upright without pain, and his arms and hands would obey him, albeit stiffly, he called for books to be brought to him. At first he only read light verse, then travel tales, then romances and other pleasant things of no import. But as

26

his strength grew and his mind awakened from its sorrows, he turned again to the study of magical lore, this time with an intensity he had never known before.

Theremderis saw that the Prince's personality had changed. His wittiness was gone. He wrote no more poetry. His broad curiosity had narrowed into an obsession with a few things.

He tried to direct the Prince's reading, to give him a balanced view of the world. He tried to ease him toward his responsibilities as lord of his people, bringing him treatises on the political arts and lecturing him on the things a ruler should know. But the young man paid only polite attention, all the while brooding, his mind far away.

"Listen, my Lord," said the wizard. "Remember that I will only rule in your place until you have your strength back. Then you must take charge. You are of age now. It is the law. I hope you'll make it possible for me to rest soon. I am very tired."

"Just now I have little taste for ruling," said Evnos.

"It is your duty. One born to so high a station as yours must put aside personal concerns, all feelings too. It doesn't matter what you *want*. You are not a commoner. You *must* fulfill your rôle, or wicked men will use you as a puppet. You will have betrayed yourself and your people. There are innumerable examples of this sort of thing in the chronicles. You know what happens to such rulers."

"Please don't recite it all now."

"Just remember that through neglect dynasties come to an end."

"Perhaps the lords of those dynasties had other interests."

"Usually the chopping block. They often found themselves there."

The Prince gazed idly out the window.

The wizard spoke in stern, hushed tones. "You *must* be *worthy* of your name. You *must* defend your throne against all dangers. *Do you understand?*"

"Yes, yes. I understand."

"I hope you will find a wife soon. After all you have been through, you shouldn't sit in your great hall alone. Also, you must have an heir."

"Do not be afraid. I'll find a wife. I'll have an heir."

Theremderis knew what he really meant, and he was very much afraid. The boy — he could never think of him as anything but a boy — had not given up on Riacinera. He was as stubborn as his father and grandfather before him. All the princes of Iankoros were like that. It led them either to glory or to disaster.

Evnos, pale and dwarfed among so many pillows, reached under the sheets and drew out a large and ancient book, bound in leather with jewel-studded boards and closed with a bronze hasp. Therem-

27

deris recognized it as the *Greatbook of Thal Adach'in*, known among the learned as the *Book of Life*.

"Profound reading you have there, my Lord. Where did you get it?"

"A serving man fetched it for me. He was so afraid of your curses that he wouldn't go unless I said magic words over him. So I solemnly blessed him and recited a recipe for soup in Sityani."

"I shall have him whipped!"

"Don't trouble yourself," the Prince sighed. "It will do no good. He was only my instrument. And, I have already read the book. You're too late."

"Well, then it would seem that the pupil has looked ahead many lessons into the future. He would know what the master knows."

"Will you explain it to me?"

"I have little choice. It is better for you to know these things completely than for you to half understand them and think you know all. That would be far more dangerous."

"I am not afraid."

The old man drew up a chair beside the bed. Together they paged through the *Book of Life*. Questions were asked and answered. Theremderis was amazed at the ease with which the Prince grasped the most abstruse concepts. He hoped that if Evnos could so easily understand all these details, he would soon grasp the overall meaning and learn the lesson the book was intended to teach. The wizard felt some relief at the prospect. But when they came to the final chapter of the book, which tells the truth about the battle between the Great Gods and Rannon and the fate of men in the first days of the world, he was again disturbed.

"Why are these lies included here?" Evnos snapped.

"They are not lies, my Lord."

"Explain."

"Perhaps we should stop. The *Book of Life* is not something to be mastered all in one day."

"I have already studied it for a long time. Tell me this, at least. Is it true that the gods did not die to redeem men from Rannon, that they did not buy our lives with their holy blood? Did they really abandon us?"

"They did."

"Why was I originally taught otherwise?"

"All men are taught so. It is a comfort, and a protection. The truth would drive them mad, or at least destroy their moral sense."

"How so?"

"If, my Prince, it were known that there is no hope in this life and no mercy in the next, if all mankind knew that Rannon takes no notice of good deeds and cannot be bribed with gifts or prayers, people would say, 'Why should we obey moral law? What is it worth, when both good men and evil suffer equally in the Underearth?' They would conclude that it is worth nothing at all, and they would abuse one another, steal what they want, and kill when they please. They would only be serving Rannon by doing these things."

"But they would have a point, philosophically at least."

"What use is philosophy if there is no happiness? The purpose of morality is to make men content in this life, to keep the peace. There can be no joy beyond the present life, so this is the only chance we have. If a lie serves such an important end, then let a lie be told. Truth is not sacred."

Evnos lay back and pondered this. The last person he had ever expected to belittle truth was Theremderis, and yet the old man had just done so.

"Is it also not correct," he asked after a pause, "that the Great Gods abandoned mankind out of contempt or disinterest?"

"Yes. So it was in the beginning. So it is now. The Great Ones care nothing for us, and have left us to fend for ourselves against Rannon. Only the lesser gods remain on Earth and they have no power over Death. They fear Rannon as we do."

"Gladziri said that."

"Why should he have lied? Superlunary beings have no concern for such matters. It is but trivia to them."

"He also mentioned something else, and I have been thinking about it for a long time." The Prince brushed hair out of his eyes and looked straight at the wizard. He spoke slowly, carefully formulating each word. "Gladziri said that to the north, near the edge of the Earth or beyond it, there is an entrance to the Underearth, an opening in the face of an enormous cliff. He said that this is a real place, a solid thing, not ethereal, and that all the funeral ships of mankind arrive there eventually."

"The land of the dead is indeed no figure of speech, no abstraction," said Theremderis. "There *is* such a place. For this reason, we never bury anyone in Iankoros, as some of the barbarians do in their own countries. Instead, we place our dead upon the sea, that they might go directly into the Underearth through the entrance Gladziri spoke of. It is said that those who do not go in the body, who are buried or cremated, and go in spirit alone, suffer even greater pains."

"Would it be possible then, for the sake of argument, if someone wanted to try it, for a *living man* to go into the Underearth and snatch someone from that place, bring them back into the our world, and restore them to life again?"

So that was it! The older man's face hardened with rage. He rose from his seat and seized the book from the Prince's hands.

"No! It is *not* possible! Don't even think of it! It should never be contemplated. It could never be done. Is Rannon such a fool?"

"Gladziri said he was."

"My Lord, the Lady Riacinera is dead forever! Forget her!"

The Prince cried out at the mention of her name, and Theremderis shared the pain. The wizard saw the need for calm, rational explanation. He reseated himself, still holding onto the book tightly.

"I can't forget her," Evnos sobbed. "I shall go mad first."

"Consider, my Lord," said the wizard, "the ways of battle. The soldiers form a shield wall against the enemy, so that each protects the other. They move in a single mass, which cannot be broken. But if one rash fellow seeks glory or something equally vain and breaks from the shield wall to run into the ranks of the foe, what do the enemy soldiers do? They laugh as they cut him to pieces, then force their way through the hole he left in his own line. Nothing has been gained and all are endangered. Likewise, if a city is besieged by overwhelming numbers, and the defenders rush out to offer battle, they are merely cut down. So with us. We are besieged by Rannon. Do you understand me?"

"Yes, I understand."

"Good. It was a foolish thing you said, spurred on by your grief. Think no more on it."

"I won't. Don't worry."

Theremderis did not believe him. The wizard left, deeply troubled.

Weeks passed and the Prince brooded. He read the books of the ancients, searching for the way to the lands of Rannon. There were no maps, but there were hints in accounts of dreams and visions. He tried to assemble these like beads on a string. As he did, he considered the warning of Theremderis, but twisted the old man's words. True, an army could not march into the Underearth, but what about a single man, moving by stealth like a thief in the night?

He Begins His Journey

WHEN PRINCE EVNOS WAS TWENTY, his time of waiting was over. Behind him at last were the long months of secret necromancies, the probings, the failures, the experiments with animals. He had called dogs, cats, birds, and even a horse back from unlife into life, and he knew as well as anyone could the techniques for restoring flesh to bones, for breathing breath back into the dead.

Still, there were no human corpses available to him. All the dead of Iankoros went to Rannon on the day of their dying. That was the tribute the Dark Lord demanded.

Much was as yet unknown.

One day in early autumn he commanded his leather-worker to sew him two bags, one small and ordinary, such as a cobbler might use to carry his tools in, and the other much wider and longer.

He bade the man deliver the bags to him in the middle of the night, paid him, swore him to secrecy with a terrible oath, and sent him away wondering.

Just before dawn he broke his fast and took up his sword, Dran. He put on a thick jerkin and winter leggings and heavy mail, a fur cape, and a polished war helm. He belted on his sword and found that, after his long convalescence, the belt was too large for him, as was his mail-coat.

He wrapped the larger of the leather bags around himself, as a soldier carries a blanket. Sweating from all this, he took the smaller bag in hand and left the castle by a secret passage.

The night air was cool on his face, but still his clothing was much too heavy. But he bore the discomfort and walked to an orchard, where he filled the small sack with fruit. It was the harvest season, early autumn, and there were apples and grapes in abundance.

This done, he set out for the Black Cliffs. The eastern sky was beginning to glow by the time he got there. The sea was still dark, the thin line of the nearby continent still invisible in the gloom. Below, feeble breakers washed over rocks. The tide was halfway out. Above, the stars faded.

Perspiring even more from the load of fruit, he made his way down the narrow, pebble-strewn path that led to the beach. At the bottom, he laid his cloak and bag down on the sand. He removed his helmet and stood in the cool air. Sweat dried on his body and he felt a slight chill.

He began his labors.

Along the shoreline he found three perfect clam shells. He laid them out end-to-end, with a twig standing upright between the first and second shells. From beyond the high-tide line, he gathered heaps of dried kelp into a pile. He snapped his fingers, said a word, and smoke wisped from the kelp. When the flames were bright, he took a wooden disk out of his pocket, an offering-coin, and cast it into the fire.

He called upon Caran Ctho, a lesser god, whose voice is the sea breeze. Likewise he invoked Yoth, the patron of Iankoros and protectress of sailors. He lied to both of them about his purpose.

"Friends, accept this offering. I want to go fishing today, far out to sea where the whales ride. Send me a wind, and I will catch it."

Almost at once, a breeze blew from the south, stirring the sand and grasses along the narrow beach. Evnos took a specially-prepared rope and bound the wind with it. Again the air was still. He laid the knotted rope on the ground. He dropped another coin into the fire.

"I thank you for the wind. Now send me a boat swifter than any made by hands."

He watched the sea shells expectantly. There came a noise like distant thunder. As it drew nearer, it became a rustling, a faint pounding. Sand whirled into the air, hiding the shells, the grains stinging his face. Only dimly could he see the shells change and grow. His eyes could not follow. He held up his hand to protect his eyes, and then saw that the shells were as big as shields, expanding as he watched. A man could sit in them. Now they fused together, became one, while their sides rose and curved. The twig was part of them now. It shot up like the shaft of a spear, like a tree.

32

When all was done and the sand once more lay still, a white boat rested at the water's edge, pale with a trace of blue, like the color of fallen snow in the earliest evening; ten cubits in length, with a mast standing two thirds of the way forward, and strange runes carved on the bow, circling around the image of a staring eye. A sail hung limp in the twilight, its silver thread gleaming faintly.

"I give you the name *Water Dove*," he said to the boat, and in that naming took mastery of it.

He threw three more coins into the fire and called upon Annan Ladin, the patron of lovers.

"Help me find my beloved," he said.

He placed rope, cloak, helmet, and both bags into the boat and pushed the craft out beyond the breakers, until the sea came to his thighs. Then he heaved himself aboard, loosened the rope a little, and the sail filled with wind. He took the tiller in hand and steered to the north. Iankoros slid away behind him in the darkness.

By the time the sun was up he was near the Amyrthelian mainland. To his left stretched reed-filled marshes, and beyond them rose forested hills. Blue, haze-masked mountains loomed in the distance. He knew those hills and those trees. The wood was called Turyin. He had fought a battle there.

By midmorning the Dawnview Hills had passed, and with them the Watchers' Hall where the priests first view the sun each day. The last of the continent's eastern arm was gone. Blue sea stretched unbroken ahead of him, beneath an almost blindingly bright sky.

By noon he was hungry, and ate a single apple from his hoard. Then he spoke aloud the secret word of the salmon's binding, and almost at once a fish leapt over the gunwale and lay wriggling in the bottom of the boat. He rose to his feet, stretched his cramped legs, and killed the fish with a quick blow of his heel. He spoke the words to command fire, and a ball of flame appeared in the air an inch above the salmon. Grease ran in the bottom of the *Water Dove*. When the fish was cooked, he touched the flame with his hand and the fire vanished like a burst bubble. He ate what he wanted, then tossed the rest of the fish to the gulls, who required no special summoning.

Hours passed. The sun was hot, the sky still clear. A few long, white clouds stretched along the horizon before him. Evnos sat still by the tiller and rehearsed in his mind the lines of the poem he was composing, his first in a very long while. It was quite different from his earlier verse, more complex, more intense in its tone. The title was *The Celebration of Riacinera*. He recited it aloud, and when a line seemed false, or the rhythm was strained, he went back and made a change, then recited again, until he felt the music of his

33

fervent expectation, his coming joy. Slowly, like a glacier sliding down out of the mountains, the poem grew.

So died the day, and in the twilight he called another fish out of the sea. It was almost dark when he passed the Isle of Nradim, the land of merchants. Once he drew near a heavily-laden galley lumbering home from some distant port. He did not wish to be seen, so drew a cloak of shadow over himself and his boat. Invisible, like a patch of darkness on the water, he drew close enough that he could hear the coarse jests of the sailors. They had come a long way and were glad to be home. Someone was waiting for each of them. Evnos wished them all well, for he knew the feeling. Someone was waiting for him too. Soon the lights of the vessel drifted astern in the night, and the island of merchants was gone.

He awoke the next morning to find the sun already risen, and a flat, straight coastline to the west again, very far away. He was not entirely sure where he was, and saw only leagues upon leagues of white beaches and pine forests beyond them, unchanging through the hours. He loosened the wind-rope a little more, gaining speed. The monotonous coastline continued without any recognizable landmarks. This had to be some part of Amyrthel, still, but he had no way of knowing how far the boat had drifted while he had slept, nor how far north he had come. The air was slightly chilly, the sky still clear.

He wove more words into his song.

He awoke in the morning twilight of the third day. The land was now very close. In the distance, beyond the trees, a white tower stood upright like a marble spear, tall, thin, windowless, and without battlements. He had come a long way indeed: he knew that tower, and the recognition was an uneasy one.

He had read of this land, and of the tower built centuries before by the wizard Abdruthim, who caused time itself to slumber around him while he and seven champions lay in beds of motionless flame awaiting the horn-blasts which shall announce the world's last day. He had read, too, of the pirate-king Vanmiri, who was cast up on that shore and sought the treasure-hoard of Abdruthim, which was reputed to be beyond any counting. But Vanmiri discovered white flowers growing in the darkest part of the forest, clustering thicker and thicker as he drew near the tower. In time the pirate grew weary; the distance to the tower seemed to stretch out forever; and he lay down in the forest and slept, never to awaken.

Evnos was not entirely sure he believed the story. How could it have been reported? But he had no intention of attempting to disprove it. He steered out to sea, giving Abdruthim's tower and forest wide berth. He loosened the wind-rope yet more, careful not to untie it all the way, lest the wind escape.

34

The Prince knew, then, that he had passed the mouth of the river Thanic during the night, and was already beyond the point where maps ended. Beyond the Thanic, cartographers merely drew in marvels.

The shape of the land itself began to change, the gentle beaches rising into fearsome cliffs. The coastline was rough, treacherous with rocks, whirlpools, and tidal blow-holes, where the water rose in roaring plumes with each breaker. It would be impossible to land a boat there.

He noticed that there were no gulls on these rocks. He called out the name of the gull clan, but no birds came. He then called on the fishes, but none came. It was a deserted place, land and sea alike, emptied by dread.

The sea rolled and heaved. The sky was steely gray.

Around noon he reached the city of Gog, called the Terror of Night. It was horrible enough by day.

It was some relief that the folk of Gog hid from the sun, for theirs was no human city. The dwellings were squat and broad, hewn of dull black stone. The towers, walls, and rooftops were formed from huge, lifelike images of human faces, the faces, it was said, of those murdered in midnight wanderings; faces that seemed still alive. Even while their masters slept, the murdered ones screamed to the open sky. They called out to Evnos, their lips flapping like limp, fleshy flags; shrieking wordlessly, mindlessly in unending fear and pain.

Evnos turned away from the sight. Surely, he thought, the builders of this city were allies of Rannon, made in his own likeness. There was much of the god's mind in that design.

He loosened the wind-rope all he dared, and the *Water Dove* leapt over the waves until the city was far behind.

He had no peace for all that day, as unnatural vistas followed one another like a parade of nightmares. Shapes rose out of the sea and sank again, twisted things larger than whales, half like men, half like nothing known to man.

To the east, a lonely rock stood against the horizon. Here was the castle of Tyan Brathe, he knew, and when he sailed past it without drawing any nearer, he was glad. Sailors told of it and philosophers dismissed the idea — and yet there it was, real enough, not built of stones at all, but tier upon tier of living, blind eyes, gazing immortally down the eons. No one knew of its origin. Talaxis Uturnir listed it in his *Described Things* as one of the great mysteries of the world.

In the Straits of Han, serpent-women lounged in the shallow waters, twitching their tails and singing alluring songs. The Prince sang his own song, the song of his beloved, until he could no longer hear them. By the strength of this and of the wind that Caran Ctho had given him, he passed through the straits and emerged into the Northern Sea beyond.

By nightfall, it was bitterly cold, the sky dark and starless. He huddled in his fur cloak and slept but little.

On the morning of the fourth day, the sea was rough and white-capped, the sky overcast, and the air colder still. Snow flurries whirled.

Breathing puffs of white mist, Evnos conjured up another fireball, this time for warmth. His teeth still chattered. Ice formed on the tiller; he chipped it off with a knife. The snow fell harder, and the world was gray and blank and quiet.

He could not see the sun to tell the hour, but knew the day was well along by the time he sighted the other vessel. At first it was little more than a speck bobbing up and down in the distance, but details slowly resolved themselves. As it neared, he made out a black longboat with a black sail. Brightly colored banners hung over the sides. He knew it for the funeral ship of a wealthy man, not royalty, not a warrior; probably a trader. The emblem of some house gleamed on the bow, but Evnos did not recognize it.

He steered the *Water Dove* alongside the death ship, tightening the knotted rope until the captive wind blew no more. Standing up, he could see over the gunwale of the other vessel. An old man lay in the middle of the deck, thin and white-haired, surrounded by sealed jars, heaps of gold, and fine silks. He had been on his final voyage for a long time already, for his face was blue-black and shrivelled, and the gulls had pecked out his eyes.

The Prince did not know the dead man's name, nor had he any wish to know it, but he was glad to see him. Here at last was a human specimen to work with. Here was a chance to truly practice his art.

He cast his cloak aside despite the cold, raised his arms and spread them apart, and began a long series of incantations, memorized from *The Book of Life* long before and many times rehearsed. He spoke all the hidden words giving power over the parts of the body, and called on the various lesser gods associated with love, comfort, and healing. He spoke of the light, and balanced it against Rannon's darkness.

By his command, the flesh grew once more on the bones. The face was covered and made whole. He drew the lips back from their curled grimace. He bound the flesh and the bone and the sinew with his words and with his will. He spoke the words of strength and of healing, while the two vessels rose and fell on the rough sea and the snow closed around them like a curtain. And the corpse was strengthened and healed.

Yet there was no breath in it.

Prince Evnos called upon the spirit of Time:

"Nanda Kanil of the Thousand Faces, who gave us evening and morning, give back the evenings and mornings of this man!"

And he spoke the true and secret name of Time, a name known only to the most select of sorcerers; aloud he spoke it until the sea and air and earth could hear it, and Time was bound. He sensed the dead man's hours hovering about him, fleeting fragments of memory that were not his own, a sunset, a foreign word spoken in the night, the taste of a cake from the oven of a mother who was a stranger to him.

Still there was no breath, and he turned to the winds, to south, to west, to east, but never to the north, for the north wind is Rannon's.

"Winds of the pure directions, hear the word of the one who binds your names. *Breathe*, winds, into this flesh that it may live, into the nostrils of this man that he may rise and stand up on his feet again. *Breathe* so that his eyes may witness again the rising and setting of the sun. *Breathe* so he may give the rousing shout. *Breathe* so that he may walk once more in his own land. *Breathe* into him, Winds, as I have commanded you. I speak your names!"

The winds came to Evnos, the winds of south and west and east with their thunder, with their roaring voices, raising great waves, shredding the sail and rigging of the funeral ship, driving the *Water Dove* away. Evnos had to grapple with the winds and master them before he could continue. After a few minutes he bound them with his words as surely as with rope, and directed them into the dead man, into the corpse's open mouth. Still the sea raged and the two vessels shook and heaved.

The winds scattered the dead man's treasure; his clothing flapped in tatters.

They breathed into him, and his lungs were filled.

He rose to his feet.

"I've done it!" Prince Evnos cried to no one. He waved his hand and the winds were silent. The waves subsided. The *Water Dove* and the funeral boat rocked uneasily, their sides a few feet apart.

The Prince watched, wordlessly, as the old man walked to the railing of his own ship and stared back at him.

The resurrected one's face was slack, expressionless. His mouth hung open.

"Hail, friend!" the Prince called out. There was no response. The old man's eyelids fluttered, then closed.

"Awake!" Evnos shouted the word of power to banish sleep, and the eyes opened once more. They were wide with terror. The man swayed from side to side, all coordination gone from his arms and legs, his hands waving like those of a puppet out of control.

"Speak!"

His mouth closed suddenly, then his jaw dropped, and he spoke, "Ggaaaahh! Gaaah!"

He leaned forward, went limp, and toppled into the sea.

There had never been a resurrection, the Prince realized. That man had never been alive, only animate, filled with wind. Something was missing. The magic did not work. His only hope was to study more, to keep trying until he had perfected the technique.

Exhausted, he slumped down by the tiller, untied the wind-rope a little, and in a short while left the empty, broken ship behind. His mind was a tangle of dread and fading triumph and uncertain expectation. He tried to add lines to the *Celebration of Riacinera*, but the words would not come.

It would be no smiling bride he brought back to Iankoros.

C The Shores of the Underearth

IN THE END it came to this: the air was damp and intensely cold, the snow no longer falling, and the shadow of Rannon stretched over the gray sea. By night the stars peered down through ragged clouds, strangers in their own sky. By day the pale glow of the sun barely lit the southern horizon.

Evnos had reached the end of the World Ocean, and the Mountains of the Edge loomed before him, holding back the waters from the abyss beyond. He huddled in the stern of the *Water Dove*, occasionally chipping ice from the tiller and rudder. He gave up conjuring balls of fire for warmth: they only went out. He had to save his energies. He was far from Iankoros, and his power was weak here.

The sea wind was a frigid blast against him, and he untied his own wind as much as he dared. The boat made slow progress, a tiny bit of flotsam against the huge cliffs ahead. They rose, terrible in the gray twilight, snow-capped and ice-sheathed, entertaining no beaches. The waves of the sea crashed against the eternal feet of the mountains.

Funeral ships were all around him now, all borne by the current in a single direction, regardless of the wind. He could see three or four at any particular moment, dark shapes tossing on the water.

The cliffs claimed their share of Rannon's tribute. By sheer strength of arm and the power of bound wind, the Prince drew away from the dark stone face, but several of the pilotless barges, the

39

larger, clumsier ones, splintered against the rocks as he watched, their treasures dumped into the hoard of the sea, their corpse-passengers left bobbing in the surf.

How many days had it been? Six? Seven? After he had sailed into the darkness, he had lost track of time. Had the faint light appeared to the south a few times while he slept? When he awoke to see a trace of pale white on the horizon behind him, he never knew for certain how long it had been there, and the fading was so gradual that he could not perceive the moment the day, if such a thing could be called day, ended. Still he knew he was near his destination.

He sailed along the rim of the world until he came to an opening in the cliffs. For a moment, when he first saw it, the gap reminded him of the harbor-mouth in Iankoros.

He made his way through a narrow channel, amid tangles of drifting funeral ships. The great vessels of princes and kings surrounded him, and the equally ornate ones of rich merchant houses, and smaller, more modest ships, barges, and even mere open boats, or the rafts of the poor. Once he passed the remains of a man, tied to a log.

At the far end of the channel, all similarity to his home isle ended. The current led him not into a harbor, but an immense cavern, dimly lit by an uncertain glow from the water, as if an impossible fire guttered far below; a cavern so huge that he could not discern the ceiling or the extent of its walls. In every direction, rotting masts and abandoned hulks stuck out of the water. Gold and jewels lay spilled on flooded decks, meaningless to Rannon.

He knew where he was. This was the Death Cave, into which all ships bearing Rannon's tribute came at last.

The air was even colder than it had been outside, and chunks of ice floated among the debris. There were thousands of corpses. The water was thick with them, almost solid in places, and the prow of the *Water Dove* pushed them aside as the vessel moved. Now Evnos tightened the knot of his wind-rope all the way, and the sail went slack. He let himself drift until he came to a tiny inlet in the side of the cave. There he moored his craft and disembarked, taking with him his sword, Dran, and the two leather bags. He put on his war helmet and stood still for a moment, surveying the vast interior harbor of the cave. Ships and the remains of ships stretched as far as he could see, into the curving, dim distance.

He found a narrow ledge and followed it around the semi-circular wall of the cavern until he came to a wide beach of white sand.

Bodies lay on the beach, piled layer after layer at the water's edge by a tide obedient to Rannon. Here were all the world's slain, all the victims of disease and the malice of chance, all those who had known terror and pain in the night and no morning after; folk of all races, all lands, many hideously maimed, limbs twisted in impossible ways. The Prince walked carefully among them, stepping over a dark-hued Bantarian who held his own severed head in frozen fingers, a maiden whose eyes had been gouged out by torturers, a blue baby, a limbless thing that might have once been a child, an old man shrivelled like a leaf.

Evnos went a long way, lost amid the endless dead, before he made out a dim shape against the back of the cavern. Only slowly, as he approached, were the details clear.

It was an enormous toad-thing, as massive as an elephant, sitting atop a flat stone. In its curiously human hands it held a flute the length of a lance.

The figure opened dully glowing eyes. Evnos froze in sudden terror.

It began to play, and he trembled at the sound.

The dead moved. Slowly, without intelligence or feeling, they propped themselves up on shattered elbows, on legs without any feet, clinging to one another in stumbling tangles of limbs and gaping faces. They trudged and wriggled out of the sea, further up onto the beach, drawn by the shrill music, forming a rough line. The tune changed slightly. Evnos felt himself impelled to follow. It took effort to remember why he was there, to avoid becoming one more mindless marcher in the great procession which was forming. Still, with deliberation and dread and sudden hope, he joined them, pulling his cloak tightly around himself to hide his armor and sword. He followed, shuffling stiffly in imitation of the others as they made their way into an opening in the cave wall behind the piper.

Soon he was in a lightless passage. The air was thick with the odor of brine and of rotting flesh. He groped in the darkness, colliding with bodies, losing all sense of direction. The dead seemed to make their way by instinct, or by some command the living Prince could not hear.

Once he stumbled and frantically grabbed the belt of some corpse, pulling himself up before he could be trampled. Then he put a hand on a cold, wet shoulder in front of him and allowed himself to be led.

After a while there came a new sound, like a wind at first, then rising to a moan from a thousand dead throats, almost a whimper, almost, too, a kind of singing, a terrible, hopeless song in time with the monstrous piping. Evnos felt a new terror then, the realization that Riacinera had endured all this. She was ahead of him, down there somewhere in Rannon's kingdom. It all became real to him, where before he had only been able to imagine: she was one of Rannon's slaves, like all these others.

What was he doing with her now?

The air gradually warmed. The stench became a nearly solid thing as the corpses began to thaw. Still they shuffled on, deeper into the realm of the dead.

Hours passed. The tunnel narrowed in places, and decayed flesh was pressed against decayed flesh; sometimes bursting, sometimes shoved into the Prince's face as all of them crowded through. It was especially in these narrow places that little unseen creatures ran chattering among the legs of the prisoners, squealing insults in countless tongues, stripping off chunks of flesh from whatever they could grab. Something bit Evnos on the ankle, right through his boot. He cursed and kicked. He dearly wanted to speak a spell for lighting, then unsheathe Dran and put an end to this, but he knew better. It had been a mistake even to kick. He had to wait, go as far as he could without being detected, or all was lost.

The man in front of him, whose shoulder he had been clutching, went down. Bones crunched. There was no cry.

After a time, Evnos was aware that he could no longer hear the piper's playing. The music had been replaced by another sound, gradually rising from a faint rumble to a thundering that filled the passage, like the speech of the god of earthquakes, like the pounding of endless waves, like the voices of all the Earth's millions raised in agony. The Prince put his hands to his ears but could not shut it out. He felt faint. His head seemed ready to split. He found himself mouthing the words of a spell to make himself deaf, and forced himself to undo it. He bit his tongue, and the sensation helped him concentrate. He needed all his awareness now, all his senses.

The tunnel widened into an open place, a room or another cavern, but far smaller than the first, with a low ceiling. Several times his helmet scraped against outcroppings from above.

The sound was worse here, reverberating from the walls, building on itself like an avalanche. The stench was worse too, the air thick and foul with what he was sure was the passage of millions of corpses over thousands of years.

Yet he could move about. He was not pressed closely. The dead milled aimlessly.

A burst of light blinded him, but when his eyes adjusted, he realized that it was actually very faint. Tapers burned in niches along the walls. He wasn't sure if he had somehow turned a corner in the dark and come within range of the light, or if the tapers had been suddenly lit.

Now he could make out dim shapes, and, nearby, their idiotic, distorted faces with their pain-filled eyes.

The sound he had heard and still heard was screaming, so loud it became a kind of pain. The very ground trembled with it.

He reached down quickly, seized a handful of mud, and plugged

42

his ears. That helped a little. The mere act of doing something helped a little.

The floor and walls were rough and bare. This was not a room, but indeed a second cavern, far underground. Miles down, he thought. It felt like miles. He stood there wondering, gasping the stagnant air.

A massive gate loomed in the darkness at the far end of the cave, white and smooth, as if carven from a single, impossible piece of bone. On either side of this, serpent-headed lions sat on pedestals, armed with glowing iron rods.

One of the dead neared the gate and stood between the two creatures. A serpent mouth spoke.

"I give you the gift of pain, the blessing of my master."

Iron touched flesh, branding it forever with the seal of Rannon. An inhuman throat laughed; a human one screamed.

The gates swung inward. All the thundering, all the screaming was coming from the other side, now immeasurably louder.

The dead man was admitted, the gate closed behind him. The relative silence was numbing.

Again iron seared flesh, and the blessing of pain was bestowed. The gate opened once more. These things happened a third time, and a fourth, and continued. Evnos understood where he was now. For all he had traveled, for all he had endured, his journey was only beginning. He was in the anteroom of the Underearth. Rannon's domain truly began beyond that gate.

Another went through, and still more. The Prince held back from the crowd, unsure of what to do next. For the moment no one was coming down the tunnel, and the cave would soon be empty.

Still hesitant, he found himself the last one remaining. Four eyes glared at him.

"You too!"

The two monsters turned toward him on their pedestals, brandishing their irons.

Evnos mimicked the listless walk of the dead as well as he could, slowly approaching the two guardians of the gate. They slid their irons into their mouths and hissed gray smoke between needle-sharp teeth, then drew the irons out again, and reached down to touch Evnos with the white-hot tips.

He flung his cape open, and Dran flashed from its scabbard.

"Brother! This one is *still alive!*"

"Brother! This one is *still alive!*"

Dran replied quickly. Two ophidian heads lay snapping at the dirt, while their bodies still squatted on the pedestals. They did not bleed.

Evnos stood there for a moment, unsure of what to do next. Dead

43

men and women began to emerge from the tunnel, filling the cave again. He turned to them and shouted, "Go back! You're free!"

But they did not turn back or make any response at all, instead milling about aimlessly, as the first group had. The Prince saw how foolish he had been. He wasted no more time. He pushed hard on the gate and swung it open.

The screaming struck him like a solid blow as he stood at the threshold of the Underearth. He reeled, almost losing his footing.

He stood atop a high ridge, looking down over dark valleys and naked hills. Here and there in the distance, great fires burned. He had no impression of being inside a cavern this time. This was another *world*. The landscape stretched as far as he could see. The air was thick with smoke beneath dirty gray clouds. The sky lacked any discernible sun, but somehow the whole land remained in endless twilight, the shadows hiding much, but often far too little.

He let the gate swing closed behind him and began to make his way carefully down a steep hillside. On ledges and in nooks, people were suffering every imaginable agony. They called out to him in hopelessness, in madness. Somehow they could sense he was not one of them, not like them. But he continued without pause, past an old man forever condemned to weave tapestries out of the flesh of his loved ones, cutting strips as they writhed and screamed; past a woman who floundered like one drowning in a pit of tiny, white-hot serpents. Even as he glanced at her, her whole body swelled and distended, then burst with a watery pop, splattering gore and venom. As he drew away, he realized that her bones and flesh were slowly coming back together, while the patient serpents waited all around her.

A head dropped down at his feet as he traversed a narrow ledge. The eyes rolled up until he could see the pupils. The mouth spoke.

"Why have you come among us, you who are truly a stranger here?"

Pebbles and stones rained on him from above. He looked up, shielding his face with his hand, and saw a headless corpse scrambling down onto the ledge. It stood in front of him, reaching for the head; but the head rolled out of its grasp, further down the hillside. The corpse followed, reaching, stumbling, the head forever just beyond its grasp.

"Why?" the head shouted. "Why?"

He stopped and stared and wept at the sight of a young girl lying among some boulders. Her legs were gone. Feasting worms swarmed over the rest of her body, while she merely lay still, whimpering, occasionally calling out a name. Most of her face had been stripped away, but the worms had not touched her eyes. She stared at the

44

Prince, with a look of knowing, infinite agony. There would be no refuge in madness for her, no release, no ending.

At the bottom of the hill, the ground leveled out, ankle-deep in ash, then rose into rolling countryside.

He had no idea how long he wandered. There was no way to tell time here. It seemed like hours, then days; then his mind faded in a haze of exhaustion and horror and he simply could not tell. He saw all the world's dead around him, all the great kings, all the soldiers, scholars, holy men, all the laborers, all the beggars, all the babies who had died before being named. All of them were tormented indiscriminately; good and evil suffered alike, not for reward or punishment, but for the mere sport of Rannon.

Riacinera never left the Prince's thoughts as he climbed over quivering, bloody hills where great masses of living flesh had fused together, no longer recognizable as individuals for all distorted faces covered the sides of raw, pink cliffs, for all arms waved like storm-tossed reeds and the very landscape screamed at his passing.

He had to harden himself, to shut out any concern for their sufferings and concentrate on his single goal, or else he would go mad.

Rannon had Riacinera. *What was he doing with her now?*

Evnos cursed the hopelessness of his own position, the crazed folly of his mission. The land was vast. It seemed endless. Its screaming denizens were without number. How then did he hope to locate just one among them?

A burning man stood at a crossroads, between two bleeding mountains. His flesh crackled furiously, like straw, little pieces drifting into the air. The Prince asked him if he knew of the Lady Riacinera.

The other only laughed. "If she is among us, she is beyond rescuing."

Evnos drew away. Overhead, winged legions flew, searching for an intruder in the land. He hurried on.

He came to a forest of folk turned halfway into trees, bound to the earth. The forest was burning as furiously as the man at the crossroads had been. Evnos walked among the people, shielded by the counter-names of fire, still choking in the foul air. He asked. No one answered. Beyond the forest, he crossed a frigid, black stream filled with ghosts, the souls of those who did not come to Rannon in the flesh. Evnos did not try to imagine what pains they suffered. He felt slimy hands reaching up, caressing his legs. All around him, ghosts moaned. The water rippled, as if they were trying to rise up, but could not. They shrieked when he climbed onto the further shore.

Next was a region of ice, then a windswept plain, then a field of stone flowers with human faces. They whispered, their voices like wind. They did not answer his questions.

But there was one among them which had fallen from its stalk.

The stone flower lay embedded in mud, like a huge dish. Evnos cleared away the center and an old woman's face gazed up at him with blind eyes. The mouth was shrunken, toothless. The lips moved slightly.

"Old Revered One, how may I find the Lady Riacinera, the Princess of Iankoros but lately come into this land?"

Nostrils flared, sucking breath. The mouth gaped open, and a voice came from within, like something shouted up from the bottom of a well, telling him to seek a lady who sat by a pool, just beyond the forest.

"Everything here, she sees. Everything," the voice cried. The stone face wept.

Evnos placed the face down gently and continued on his way. He found the woman by the pool. She sat on a flat rock, leaning over on her hands, gazing into the water. As he drew nearer, he saw that the lower half of her body was stone, fused with the rock, and her arms, too, were stone up to the elbows. She could not turn away or even change her position.

"Honored One," the Prince said in a low voice.

"Why do you call me honored? No one is honored here." She did not turn her head as she spoke.

"Lady, I —"

"I saw you in the forest. I saw you at the entrance to this land. I know what you want. I will help you if I can. I know where Riacinera is."

"Then tell me!"

"But first, you must do a favor for me, something I have longed for."

"Anything, Lady. Anything I can do . . . but *here* . . . what *can* I do for you?"

"For a thousand thousand years I have gazed into this pool. My torment is to view the torments of all the others, without end. I see them all, in these waters. I want you to put out my eyes."

The Prince took her by the hair to raise her head, but her neck and shoulders were stiff and he could not move her. So he crouched down, drew his sword, and very carefully pressed the point of the blade into one lidless eye, then into the other. Blood ran down the woman's pale face, mingled with tears.

"Thank you . . . I thank you more than any words can say. I am sure they will grow back, but I shall always remember this respite."

Then slowly, weighing each word, she told him how to find Riacinera. He felt only further, resigned dread when he had fully heard of his wife's situation. His sojourn in the Underearth was beginning to numb him even to the sufferings of his beloved. He wondered, abstractly, if he would ever recover and have the emotions of a normal man again.

"Lady," he asked gently. "Can I see her in this pool? You said you could see everything."

"No. *Don't look*. You won't be able to turn away. You'll become as I am."

"Again, I thank you."

He rose to leave. Suddenly the air was filled with flapping wings.

"What is happening?" asked the blind woman.

Evnos had no time to answer. The soldiers of Rannon had discovered him at last. They circled above, then began to descend, their huge, metallic wings whirring, blowing up dust, their feet touching the ground gently.

Their bodies were metal too, thin as skeletons, covered with black flesh drawn tight, like leather drawn tight over iron rods. Each had a single, glowing eye, and below it the whole of the face consisted of a sharp, bulging beak which opened and closed constantly, hissing and scraping.

Their swords were long and thin, like rapiers of bone. Evnos knew that even Dran could not prevail against those weapons, for they were made of Rannon's very body, and their touch was death itself.

The creatures landed in a circle around him and stepped slowly forward. The Prince turned to right and to left. There was no escape.

Then he remembered the bag of fruit he was carrying and what it was for. He reached in and threw apples on the ground.

"Here, brave ones! The gifts of earth!"

At once the creatures fell to fighting among themselves over the fruit, for they craved it. Over the centuries, as Gladziri had explained, the tormented had a way of revenging themselves on their jailers by describing to them in endless, exquisite detail the pleasures of the upper world, which Rannon's creatures of course would never know.

Pale swords flickered until only one monster remained, gorging itself on the fruit. Thus Prince Evnos escaped them for the first time. When another band found him, he did the same thing, and again for a third, using the fruit sparingly.

Beyond a curving line of upright stones stretched a plain of white matter, soft, foul-smelling, featureless. The Prince's feet sank into it; and clouds of even fouler stuff, perhaps spores, rose from his footprints. He could never quite define what the stuff resembled. It was soft, damp, as crumbly as rotted wood, or slimy, like moldering cheese. The odor was that of putrefaction, and the plain went on as far as he could see. He got out a scarf and tied it over his nose and mouth, but that helped little. He hurried on.

After a while the stuff began to bubble and rise. It was harder to walk on now. His footing was uncertain, the air thicker with dust. Once he slipped and fell and his hand touched the ground. He wiped it furiously on his cloak. The sticky feel of the substance was somehow more horrible than either the sight or the smell.

Before him, a great bubble rose, forming into a head, shoulders, two arms bursting up.

"Stay with us," the thing cried out. "You are a slave of Rannon now. There are far worse dooms than becoming one of us."

The thing reached out. Evnos jumped back and struck with Dran. The sword passed through the creature without any resistance, and there was only a cloud of the evil dust.

On he went, opposed by many, reducing them to dust as he had the first, until, finally, he noticed that the ground sloped upward. He was climbing a hill. The air was almost opaque with dust. Something touched him on the leg and he struck in every direction with his sword, frantically.

At last he saw what the woman by the pool had bade him seek. The top of the hill was shaped into a living thing, a giant visible from the waist up, as tall as a castle's tower, bloated in the belly like a toad, paste-colored, with the face of an idiot. The face loomed above him in the swirling dust, in the dim twilight of the Underearth. As he watched, the monster raised a bottle to its lips. The bottle was as big as the *Water Dove* and made of transparent glass. Inside, someone struggled in the thick liquor.

He heard screams from within the bottle and he knew the voice.

"You! Stop!" He stood before the giant and waved Dran.

The creature put down the bottle and leaned over, its face like the face of the moon half veiled by clouds. Its voice thundered.

"Who *dares*? I am Kanatekelei, son of Rannon. Who commands me to stop?"

"Down here! Down here, fat-face!"

At last the giant saw Evnos, smiled, then laughed. The whole landscape convulsed, rippling like blubber. The ground swayed and heaved beneath the Prince's feet.

"So! You are the new toy Father sends. I shall play a game with you. I shall eat you and excrete you and eat you again, and again, and again as long as it amuses me." Once more the giant laughed. Oily fluid poured from its mouth.

Evnos made no effort to dodge the warty, swollen hand that reached for him.

"Wait just a minute," he said, and the hand paused. "I know another game. Will you play it with me?"

The hand withdrew.

48

"A game with you? This is a new thing, and I like it." The giant giggled. Spittle splashed from its chin. "What sort of game?"

"A game to see who is smarter."

"Ho! A riddle! What shall I guess then?"

"Many things, to the limits of your great cleverness. But first — but first! — a gift!"

"What?"

"Behold!" The Prince's hand plunged into the sack, drawing out apples, pears, figs. "The fruits of the upper world! Fresh! Juicy! Enjoy them!" He scattered the fruits over the ground.

Again the landscape heaved, as Kanatekelei reached clumsily about, gathering up the fruit. Prince Evnos ran to where the bottle had rolled between two lumps of the godling's flesh, caught hold of the lip, and crawled into the neck, gapping at the noxious fumes from within. His hands slipped on the glass. Filth washed over him.

Something splashed in the darkness ahead, in the body of the bottle. Someone moved.

"Dearest Riacinera? Is it you?"

At first, there was only weeping as a reply.

"Yes . . . it is I. How did you come to this place so soon? So *soon*? I had hoped you would live long and be happy."

"I am still alive. Please, believe me. I could never be happy, so I have come for you. Come with me now, into the light, so that I may see your face again."

He heard more splashing footsteps receding from him. The bottle rolled and heaved. He slid forward to the inner extremity of the neck, frantically trying to avoid falling face-first into the slime.

"Beloved!" he whispered. "Hurry! Come with me!"

"It is useless," she said. "This is the greatest of my sorrows now, that you should have come all this way for me, but uselessly. Go back, my dearest one. Escape while you can. Do not look on me as I am now, for Death has touched me, and there are worms in my face."

"This is a thing I had feared."

Evnos swung his legs around and dropped into the main part of the bottle. He waded, knee deep in oily fluid, swaying from side to side precariously as the bottle moved, groping in the darkness until he found Riacinera. She let out a little cry. Her flesh was cold and hideously soft. He unwound the longer bag from around his waist and drew it over her, until she was entirely within. Then he tied it shut and hoisted her onto his shoulder. When he emerged from the bottle's mouth, the giant was still slapping its huge hands around, searching for more fruit.

The Prince ran across the rippling, trembling land, bent under

49

the weight of Riacinera. He was through the curving line of stones, onto solid ground, before he heard the giant bellow.

"Little man! You cheat me! You have not played the game yet!"

Kanatekelei snorted with rage and strained to break free of the hill out of which he had been formed. Evnos glanced back once, then again, as great fissures spouted black fluid. Dust rose like smoke from a vast fire. One monstrous leg appeared, with a half-formed foot; and another leg, and the giant stood up uneasily, leaving a huge, oozing hollow where it had been. It lurched forward, fell, and rolled down the hill. At the bottom, it rose to its feet again and lurched after the fleeing Prince.

Evnos scattered a trail of fruit behind him as he went. He heard Rannon's idiot son thrashing among the stone flowers, grubbing for more. Stems shattered. Stone petals flew through the air.

By the time he reached the other side of the forest and had re-crossed the black, whispering river, the Prince was far ahead of Kanatekelei.

For a few brief minutes he was free of pursuit. He slowed to a walk and spoke loving words to Riacinera, but she barely stirred. She mumbled something he couldn't make out. He did not open the sack.

On he went, through winds, through ice, through fire. Kanatekelei drew near once more, howling. The Prince encountered the winged guardians and left them to fight over a piece of fruit — only one piece, because his supply was running low. Sometimes he fought briefly, Dran snapping those terrible bone rapiers, hurling one metal creature onto another. Sometimes he hid among the suffering damned while the sky was black with squadrons, and the sound of their wings was like thunder. At last he came to that final cliff and climbed it. He passed the woman among the burning serpents, the girl eaten by worms, the other victims he had seen before. Now they were only landmarks, welcome milestones on the way, while their agonies had begun yet again.

Groups of newly-arrived dead fell down the slope, their limbs snapping on rocks. He dodged them as he would falling stones and struggled on.

At the top, the door was just closing. He forced it open. The two serpent brothers turned to meet him, wielding their irons. Their heads had regrown, but were smaller, neckless.

Dran crashed through their skulls, cleaving.

He forced his way up the tunnel, shoving his way through crowds of walking corpses, gagging when he got a face full of putrid flesh. Imps came out at him, but this time he *did* speak a spell for light and his face glowed like a lantern. He saw them now, dark, ragged creatures with stick-like limbs and sharp claws. Dran broke them into brittle pieces, one by one.

Then the tunnel shook with the snorts and howls of Kanatekelei. Evnos could hear bones cracking, stone falling as the dead were mashed against the tunnel walls. His enemy was very near.

Once he looked back and saw the godling filling the whole tunnel, pulping the hapless dead as it wriggled forward like some enormous worm, but then it was caught at a narrow juncture and left struggling, furiously scraping at the tunnel walls, hurling corpses aside as they blundered on their way.

Evnos burst out onto the beach again, ran past the piper who paid him no heed, then turned once more and took in the whole scene. The giant was pouring out of the tunnel mouth, its body liquescent, its flesh raw, oozing black where it had torn itself free.

The piper piped. The multitudes rose from the water's edge. Kanatekelei was no more than a spear's throw away. The Prince forced his way through the crowd, dumped the rest of the fruits in the surf and threw away the bag. He gained the ledge and made his way back to the *Water Dove*. The way seemed much farther, going back.

The son of Rannon squatted on the shore, hurling aside his father's newly arrived slaves, splashing about for more fruits.

Evnos cut the mooring line with a stroke of his sword and dropped Riacinera into the bottom of the boat. He crouched in the bow, reached out, and pushed off from the rocks, then crawled back to the stern and sat at the tiller. He waited tensely while the boat drifted clear of the inlet. Then he loosened the knot in the wind-rope as far as it would go and the sail filled. The *Water Dove* raced out of the great cave, into the channel, weaving among wrecks and incoming funeral ships.

When he reached the open sea, he realized that his face was still covered with the foul-smelling scarf. He choked, took it off, and threw it into the sea.

But he was not yet free. Behind him, Kanatekelei shouted. An enormous splash followed. The water heaved up.

The son of Rannon was following him, he knew, walking on the ocean floor.

So it was that Prince Evnos escaped from the Underearth and accomplished something no hero of old had ever attempted. At the time, he had no chance to think about the uniqueness of his deed. He sailed ever onward, back, back over the distance he had come, out of the cold and the darkness, into the light, toward the lands of living men. His heart was filled with hope and with love, and with longing for Riacinera. He could have no doubts now. He had won. He must hope and be true to his hopes.

51

Once he had carried her out of the land of the dead, the Princess never stirred in the sack, for she was not yet of the living, and the animation which Rannon grants to his subjects was gone from her. She was merely a corpse. She awaited her husband's sorceries.

The *Water Dove* passed again by wondrous and terrible lands. In the Straits of Han the ladies called out in vain, recoiling as Kanatekelei followed after. The Prince went by the city of Gog by night this time, and unseen things hissed and tittered beyond the gunwales, but the wind held steady and the boat sailed swiftly on.

Rain and storm pursued him all the way, waves crashing against the vessel, raising it, hurling it forward. An ordinary hull might have been crushed, an ordinary mast snapped, but the *Water Dove* survived. All the while the Prince sat sleepless at the tiller, never once giving in to the temptation to open the sack and look at Riacinera.

At last he saw Nradim in the distance, and the Dawnview Hills passed. Then Iankoros was a dark shape on the cloudy horizon. The island was home, but the Prince was not returning there as much as he was setting out again, on a new quest of deepest magic. Once more his journey had barely begun. At the end, Riacinera would be restored to him.

Behind him, far beneath the waves, the son of Rannon followed. Evnos was not afraid. He chanted lines of poetry aloud, composing as he did.

The Celebration of Riacinera was rapidly turning into an epic.

The Black Cliffs Again

IT WAS MIDMORNING on a damp and windy day when he reached the Black Cliffs. The air was unseasonably cold, but to one who had just returned from the farthest north, it was comfortable enough.

The sea was rough, white-capped with foam, the tide as high as it ever got, the beach reduced to a thin strip of sand and stones at the base of the glistening cliffs. Evnos climbed out of the boat into waist-deep water and dragged the vessel between two boulders. He spoke a word of thanks to the gods and the *Water Dove* was no more. A wave broke over the boulders, then poured out between them, sending shells clattering back into the depths.

He unknotted his rope and his captive wind whirled around him for a moment, angry, yet delighted to be free, and then it was gone. The Prince coiled the rope carefully, pocketed it, and took up the heavy leather sack over his shoulder, making his way up a narrow path along the edge of the cliff face. At the top, he set his burden down and waited.

Kanatekelei arrived about an hour later. The waves leapt suddenly, as if recoiling from him, crashing against the cliffs. High above, Prince Evnos felt the spray against his face and knew that it was time. He drew his sword calmly.

The ocean heaved. A familiar, misshapen head rose out of the green-gray water, into the pale daylight. Then the whole upper half of the giant emerged, dully white like the underbelly of a fish, even more repugnant now that Evnos could see it clearly. The son of the Great God lumbered onto the beach, dropped to his knees, sniffed about where the *Water Dove* had dissolved back into shells, then stood up, surveying the whole area, puzzled.

"Hey! Fat-face! Up here!" Evnos leaned over the ledge of the cliff, waving Dran.

Kanatekelei grunted in surprise, then snarled, baring yellowish stubs of teeth.

"Here I am!" the Prince cried. "I have no more presents for you but the edge of my good sword. Do you want to play a *new* game?"

The godling turned toward the gleaming blade and roared. Sea birds fluttered from the cliff in terror. Kanatekelei broke into a run, wobbling on huge strides, and was directly beneath Prince Evnos with surprising speed. Flabby, huge hands gouged deep holds into the black stone, sending splinters clattering down.

A moment later the son of Rannon stood on the cliff top and loomed over this mite who had dared to steal from the flesh-hoard of the Underearth and now shouted brave words.

Kanatekelei laughed.

Then he paused, befuddled, when the little man laughed back.

Prince Evnos savored his certain triumph then, the triumph of his own cleverness over the sheer stupidity of Kanatekelei. The monster did not seem to realize that here, on this island, so far to the south and high above the death-sacred sea, he was beyond the immediate protection of his father. Rannon, of all the gods, was endlessly patient and *most*-powerful, but not *all*-powerful. Now the balance was even, the death-god's influence at its weakest, while Evnos stood on his own home ground, wielding Dran, which Elthanoe the dwarf-king had wrought from the stones of this same island.

At this one instant, Prince Evnos and the son of Rannon faced one another as equals.

And the Prince was by far the cleverer.

The godling's laughter suddenly turned into screams of rage and pain as Dran bit through his ankles. Down he came, howling, thrashing, in a quivering, almost shapeless heap, one foot gone. Then his head rolled. His open neck spewed pus. Arms and legs flopped like beached fish, and the body wriggled like some enormous, blind, maimed spider until at last it was still.

The Prince stood a safe distance away until he was sure the giant was dead. Then he cleansed Dran in the earth and slid the sword gently back into his scabbard. He regarded his fallen foe and smiled.

"This was exceedingly well done," he said aloud.

Sack over his shoulder, he turned toward the castle. When he arrived there, he entered by the main gate and ordered the astonished sergeant on duty to collect a dozen men and go to the Black

Cliffs, where a certain thing was to be *buried* rather than thrown into the sea as custom would normally have it.

"Lord, what is it?" the man asked.

"Some refuse, only. It will be obvious enough when you get there. Take more men if you need them, but make all swear to tell no one what they have seen.

"It shall be done," the sergeant said, nodding. "May I inquire, Lord, where you have been this past week?"

"On an affair of state," said the Prince. He hurried past the sergeant before the man could ask anything more.

It was always dark inside the Tower of Eagles. The winding staircase rose into the windowless gloom, and no torches burned along the walls. When Evnos was a child, Theremderis had told him that Night slept in the bottom of the tower, resting until it was time to go out and cover the world again.

Now the Prince climbed the familiar stone steps, taking three at a stride. He went briskly, confidently, eager to get on with his work. He strove to keep his mind busy, to fill it with other thoughts, so the intensity of his love for Riacinera would not overwhelm him. It was a time to *do* rather than to feel.

So he climbed, carrying her, remembering his first long climb up these stairs. He laughed at the memory, too loud, nervously, then fell silent. The trapdoor was just above him.

He whistled a few bars of a hymn to Spring.

The trapdoor rose at his spoken command, as if lifted by an invisible hand. He spoke another word to make light, but saw that there was no need.

The upper chamber was already lit. Zio Theremderis waited for him, seated over a book, looking exactly as he had that first time. Suddenly the Prince felt very young again, very vulnerable.

"Welcome back, my Lord," the wizard said. There was no emotion in his voice.

"Hello," Evnos said without pausing. He quickly but carefully set his burden down beside Theremderis's desk. In the middle of the floor were still visible traces of circles, names, old memories.

The old man closed his book and looked up.

"My pupil — I mean, my Prince." He smiled at his apparent mistake, and then the smile faded. "This is a mighty thing you have done."

"I suppose so. But I was much too busy doing it to think about it."

"No hero has ever attempted such a feat before, much less accomplished it. It is without precedent in all the chronicles."

"Then we'll have to write some new chronicles, won't we? But later. Right now I haven't the time."

55

"I am greatly afraid of what those writings will say."

Evnos glared at him. *"What is that supposed to mean?"*

Theremderis pretended sarcasm, but with an undertone of sorrow.

"What? You don't know? Or haven't you had the time to think about it?"

The Prince ran both hands through his hair, then paced the length of the room. He faced a bookshelf, whirled around, and spoke, his voice shrill. He sounded like a boy again.

"No I don't know — I mean, *yes*, I do — Please. There is so much to prepare. I need your help more now than ever before. I need you to help me — to —"

He couldn't bring himself to say what he meant, but pointed at the bag on the floor by the desk.

"I cannot do it," Theremderis said sadly.

"What?" The Prince's voice was deeper again. He was trying to command.

"Such a thing as you contemplate is impossible," the wizard said. "I haven't the power. No one does."

"By all the gods of jesters and fools and moonstruck old ladies, *that* is a lie! A monstrous, traitorous lie! *I* am nearly able to do it. With more study, with more work, I could do it all by myself. I have brought animals back from the dead. A horse even! Did you know that? I restored a horse back to life. And when I was at sea, I tried it on a *man*. It almost worked. He rose. He walked. So, if I can just *refine* the technique a little — and if we work together, surely —"

Theremderis shook his head.

"My Prince, you don't understand. You still have learned so very little. *Animals* have no spirit. It is easy with them. You can raise up the *flesh* of a man, too. I imagine your corpse tottered impressively. But it was still dead, was it not? You did not bring back the person that corpse had been. To restore your lady's soul back into her body, to truly bring her back, is a thing we cannot do, not alone, not together, not with the help of every mighty wizard, every witch in all the lands. *No.* It would mean opposing Rannon on his home ground, in the area of his greatest strength, in *death*."

The Prince struck out angrily, sweeping books from a shelf.

"Can't means you *won't!* You mean that you *refuse* to help me. Why? Are you *afraid?"*

"My Prince, I am very much afraid. More so than I have ever been in my life."

"You're afraid I'll be better than you. Is that it? *I* will be the greatest magician in the world. Where will that leave you? Useless!"

"I do not fear for myself. I am old. I don't matter. But for you, Prince Evnos, I fear intensely."

"Will you help me?"

"No."

"Can't you see that I love her? Are you too blind and senile to recognize that?"

"Love is not enough. Rannon is stronger."

"I *order* you, as your legal sovereign, to assist me in this task. I don't want to do it this way. I have never commanded you before. But you *are* my subject, just like everyone else. I do what I must."

The wizard sat still. He folded his hands, unfolded them, folded them again, let his beard brush over them, and stared down at his crossed thumbs. After a long pause, he said slowly, "My Prince, with great regret I must disobey the first order you have ever given me, for it is a rash one and a dangerous one. You have not considered where this thing will lead you. I think that you will destroy yourself and perhaps all of Iankoros with you. I trained you, yes, and you were a bright pupil, but I fear that you have acquired no wisdom at all. You have none. You show none. You are too self-centered for that. Always, I have watched over you, protected you, even when you were no longer a child. I see now that you remain a child in many ways. You are still standing by the window making pigeons vanish from rooftops. I will not assist you. I cannot bring myself to participate in your undoing."

Evnos screamed, "If you don't obey me, *I'll have your head!*"

His teacher looked at him and asked quietly, "Would you really do that?"

The Prince said nothing. He stared at the floor. He trembled, holding back rage and tears. He did not know what to do. The choice was before him — Theremderis or Riacinera, his past or his future, wisdom or love.

At last he whispered hoarsely, "Leave me. Get out. I forget your name. I don't know you anymore."

Zio Theremderis rose silently. His footsteps were soft as he walked around his desk to the trapdoor. He didn't look back as he descended the stairs.

Only when he was outside in the courtyard did he begin to weep.

The Prince's joy was gone. He had been exultant at his feat — he *had* thought about it and rejoiced in it — but now he felt empty, afraid, alone. He had cut himself adrift from the only person he had ever looked to for security. He was entirely on his own now, and he knew that it would have to be his magic alone which would restore Riacinera, or none.

But he had to continue. Love had brought him this far. There was no turning back.

That was the answer. He had failed to resurrect the man on the ship because he had not cared the slightest bit about him. That

57

particular corpse was had been a mere object, part of an experiment, like the work with cats and dogs. He had not even known the man's name, or, in his arrogance, attempted to learn it, and without a name, any magic was surely weakened.

But this time he would not be weakened. This time he knew the subject's name. This time he loved her, and he was in his own tower, in the heart of his own kingdom, where his strength was the greatest. He had Theremderis's books and equipment to help him. But mostly he had love. His magic was love. That was the true power, which would make the difference.

Theremderis had been wrong. It *could* be done. Rannon's influence was weak here. Had not the pig-headed god's own *son* been slain on this very isle, and Rannon made no effort to aid him? Now the Lord of Death was to be conquered yet again, and the soul of Riacinera snatched from his grasp.

The Prince sat at the desk for a while, turning precious volumes to marked places, reviewing certain aspects of many arts, all things concerned with the restoration of strength, the rekindling of spirit. He went over the spells one last time to make sure he had them right in his mind, and then he knew that further reading was only an excuse to delay. He was ready.

He cleared the floor, but drew no figures on it for protection. The one he would conjure up this time was a friend, not an enemy. The shadows deepened in the room as he prepared for his labor. He glanced out the window once and saw the orange-red sun sliding behind a rooftop.

He laid the corpse out flat, still in the leather sack, then began to write on the floor around it, dipping a brush into a jar of paste made from the ashes of the phoenix, that royal bird which was the emblem of his house. He traced out the name Riacinera Rae Karavasha Ke Evnos Iankorosim, and he wrote the true name of the blossom after which she had been named, coupling that with his own inner, true name, and the true name of Iankoros itself, followed by the lines he had composed in her honor on an evening that now seemed so very long ago:

Empty perches high above.
Gone the eagle, gone the dove,
Together they are bound in love —
They've flown the whole world over.

He scattered rose petals over the floor, petals from roses grown eons before when the world was young and kept fresh in bottles by charms. He stood nineteen candlesticks in a circle around all he had written, naming each of them for his Princess's years, and he kissed them one by one and lit them with a whisper of his breath. The candles were scented and filled the room with a sweet odor.

At last, when all was ready, he opened the book with the iron hasp, the *Greatbook of Thal Adach'in* written in that sage's own handwriting. He took it, the *Book of Life*, and read aloud from it the words of life, naming the inner names of the principal living things, speaking the words first pronounced by Morosa Etewah on the Earth's first day. He spoke these words and reached out with them, with his mind, and with his hands, not into the darkness of the outer spaces, but into the soul of Riacinera — and for an instant it seemed that his hands touched hers, and her touch was soft and warm and alive.

He drew her back, into love, into life, saying, "Rise up. Rise up my love and come away. Let not your feet be still any longer. Let not your hands lie cold. Open your eyes, my love, and come away. There is still tang in the sea and blue in the skies above. Rise up. Rise up and come away. Rise and sing a song of joy, for you are brought up out of the darkness into the light, from sorrow into delight, from the stillness of sleep into the wakefulness of dance. Rise up, as I summon you, for I speak the words of life and call you by your truest name, which is *Beloved.*"

And she rose. The bag stirred and twisted. Evnos put down the book and ran to her. He untied the strings and yanked the sack away.

Riacinera lay before him as he had always known her, fresh and beautiful. She rose to her feet. There was a great light shining all about her, filling the room, dazzling his eyes.

And yet she did not speak. Her own eyes opened, but there was no sign of recognition.

"Sing!" cried Evnos. "Sing for joy! Sing the verse I have written. Sing it with me!"

He began to sing, bellowing the lines, but stopped when he realized that he was singing alone.

Her mouth fell open and she gurgled, *"Gone, ggggg . . ."*

"Beloved, it is I!"

She did not know him. The light faded. Her skin shrank in on itself, wrinkling, darkening to blue-black. She tumbled forward, scattering the candles.

His words became screams as he reached out for her, with his hands, with his love, with his magic. His whole body shook as he wrestled with great words, great spells, with the hand and grasp of Rannon.

And his power was like a brief candle in an endless cavern, a flickering speck against the eternal darkness. After a while, it went out.

The White Isle

ZIO THEREMDERIS left the castle by the back gate, saying no word to the guards there. The night was very still. His cane tapped hollowly as he crossed the wooden drawbridge. When he reached soft ground, the only sounds were the cries of night birds.

He made his way west, following the long axis of the island, away from the harbor, in the general direction of the Black Cliffs. He passed through a grove of trees, crossed a field whispering with grain in the faint breeze, then came among trees again. At one time, he reflected, all Iankoros had been forested, but then open spaces were cleared for villages and crops. Still, the remnants of the ancient forest lingered at the edge of human habitation, waiting for the time when the axes would be forever silent.

He emerged again at the edge of a field of wheat that rippled like the sea in the bright moonlight and paused in the shadows at the forest's edge. Someone laughed nearby.

A youth and a maiden sat on a boulder the farmer had never been able to remove. They giggled and passed a bottle back and forth. The young man gulped, coughed, and the liquor glistened down his chin in the moonlight.

"To life!" he shouted. "I drink to our life together. It will be nothing but joy."

"There will be hard times also," the maiden said softly, "mixed in with the joy. Life is like that."

The youth took her face in his hands and drew her gently forward until their noses almost touched.

"With you my days shall be an unending joy, one golden hour after another until the ending of time. Don't listen to what other people say. They don't know anything. Neither do I, but I *feel* it, and I know that we will always be all right, Listen: we'll have one strong child after another, until the island is completely populated with them. We'll rename the place the Isle of Ladereth's kindred. I'll be king and you will be queen."

"Oh," she said, pushing him away, laughing lightly. "That's treason."

He took her in his arms. "If it's treason, I say enjoy, enjoy."

"What would the Prince say?" she asked in mock seriousness.

"I don't think he'll notice. He doesn't come around much anymore. When was the last time anyone saw him? So, we just won't tell him."

She made no reply. The two of them kissed and lay together, flat on the boulder.

Theremderis withdrew into the woods and wandered on until he came out another way. He shook his head sadly.

He crossed a field left fallow and climbed a low, rolling hill. Back to the east, the castle was only a cluster of lights among the stars. The Tower of Eagles stood well above the others, a single open window at the top alight like a glaring red eye. The wizard knew that Prince Evnos was conjuring. Yet the night was still. It was a different kind of conjuring this time, quieter, more subtle, and yet a terrible thing.

Somewhere in the distance a drover was herding cows in from late pasture, singing a song of earth and of green, living things amid the ringing cowbells. Theremderis listened to the faint sound of the drover's voice well after he could not longer make out the words. He knew that the herdsman had found contentment, that the great events of the world never troubled him.

The wizard wanted, more than anything else, to be like that man. He would gladly give up all his power, all his learning, his authority, just to walk the dusty roads of the world and camp by their side each night, to rise again in the morning and walk, and sing, and camp again. And one morning, he knew not when for all it would certainly not be far away, he would not rise, and his sleep would go on forever. His bones would lie by the edge of the road. Perhaps other wanderers would muse over them, but they would not trouble themselves for long. That would be all, the end of Zio Theremderis — and he knew it was impossible, every detail of his fantasy. Rannon would never allow it, for the god of the dead gave his subjects no rest. And Prince Evnos would not allow it, for some fire burned in the heart of the youth, something no old man, wizard or otherwise, could hope to comprehend or control.

He thought of his life with the boy. He had lived a long enough life before the Prince was even born, but that didn't matter now. His life began over again with Evnos. But when the pupil of Theremderis became a man and ruler of isle, something had intruded. Somehow, subtly, the wizard and the student had parted ways.

The Prince who conjured in the Tower of Eagles now was a stranger. He resembled someone Theremderis had once known, but he was not the same person. The wizard had loved that boy and the boy had loved him, but who was this other? He was someone who would not hear the words of reason, of calm advice, who thought himself enough of a god to wrestle with the only god of any consequence. He was someone who had, incredibly, succeeded in the unthinkable, but was still only *beginning* to do what he had set out to do. He was a madman about to bring on disaster, the doom of all Iankoros.

That Prince Evnos remained, in his own way, as innocent as he had been on that first day when he had unwittingly magicked a pigeon out of existence did not matter. That his motives were pure, that he was driven by all-consuming love for the Lady Riacinera was of no account. In the universe of Rannon there was no such thing as innocence. Good and evil were not weighed in the balance. There were no excuses.

The end had come. Theremderis knew that this was his dusty roadside, from which he would not rise. He could shout endless warnings, but the will of Rannon was active in these events, clearly, working some inscrutable revenge, and soon lovers, herdsmen, princes, wizards and the very name of Iankoros would be swept away.

The old man assumed the failing had been within himself. He had neglected to instill in the boy a proper humility, a true understanding of mankind's lowly place in the scheme of things. He had lectured on the evils of pride, but not enough. Because of this, the Prince lacked the foresight to understand where his actions would lead. Evnos thought his great adventure nearly finished, the heroic experiment close to its resolution.

But Theremderis knew better. A little man had pinched a god. A mouse had assaulted a dragon, and for the moment escaped unharmed. But the vengeance of the dragon would be terrible, and as inevitable as the sunrise.

As if to bear witness to this, the dawn came. The wizard had walked throughout the night, far from the castle, to the other end of the island, lost in his thoughts. Then the stars faded and the sea beyond the shadow of Iankoros began to glitter. Birds awoke in the trees and began to sing.

He came to the last village, very near to the Black Cliffs. No more than a dozen wooden and stone huts lined a single muddy street. Two or three barns tottered behind the huts, and crude fences snaked across brown, rocky fields.

Sleep-eyed milkmaids met him with astonished stares.

"A wizard! Here!" The words were whispered, and shutters creaked open a crack, expectant of miracles.

Finally a girl of no more than four, with dirty feet and uncombed hair, ran out into the middle of the street, planted herself firmly before Theremderis and said, "Are you *really* a wizard?"

He nodded.

"Can you do magic?"

"Yes."

"Can you do *anything?*"

"No, not anything."

The girl was puzzled. "I thought wizards could do anything."

Theremderis smiled. "No, but we can do enough to keep ourselves busy."

"Can you . . . make money?"

"What?"

"Gold. Make me a gold coin. A shiny new one."

"Young lady, you have learned the ways of the world far too soon." He sighed, then laughed. "Very well. Hold out your hand."

She did, and he passed his own hand over hers. He said a word and there was a large gold coin in her palm, a newly minted Royal, with the profile of Prince Evnos on it.

"Oooh! Real gold!" The child ran off without bothering to thank him and knocked on a door. "Mommy! Look! Real gold!"

She stopped suddenly. The coin had disappeared. She gaped at her empty hand, then turned to Theremderis.

"Where is it? Give it back!"

"It never was anywhere. An illusion. That is all."

"You're not a real wizard! You can't do anything at all!" She pounded on the door again and began to sob. The door opened and a hand hastily yanked her inside. A woman stood in the doorway, glaring.

Theremderis couldn't find anything to say. He walked on through the village in silence. He felt old and useless. At last he came to the Black Cliffs and to the grave of Kanatekelei, a great mound of bare, upturned earth like a scar on the face of the island.

He prodded the grave with his cane.

"I might not be a real wizard," he muttered aloud, "but this is real enough, and I fear it."

He looked to the north and felt a sudden shiver of helpless dread. Somewhere beyond the world's edge Rannon sat, waiting until the time was exactly right, until the events had come together like the last interlocking piece of the terrible puzzle which would be his revenge. Prince Evnos had been a fool to put any faith in Yoth or Caran Ctho, or any of the other little gods. They were like paper boats in a tempest, less than utterly insignificant, their very existence denied.

Theremderis spoke aloud again, to the mound.

"Tell me, what does your father intend? You may confide in me. I have no power to stop him."

The mound began to rise, so slowly at first Theremderis thought it was a trick of his eyes, but rise it did, like a great beast beginning to breathe. Clods of earth fell at his feet.

"Enemy of us all — what is this?"

The grave heaved. Sand and stones poured from its sides. Theremderis stepped back, staggering. The grave-mound was already twice the size it had been. Still it stirred, writhed, mud pouring out like pus from a wound.

Theremderis waved his hands and his cane, speaking spells, calling on the powers of the air, on those same little gods Prince Evnos had so foolishly relied upon.

It accomplished nothing. The action wasn't even slowed. The earth began to shake. Gulls rose from the Black Cliffs, shrieking, startled.

He hadn't expected to be able to do anything. There was no name to call upon here. He had no power. He only shouted and waved for the comfort of doing something.

Still the mound grew, swelling out from its sides, spitting up stones. Once more Theremderis invoked Yoth, the protector of Iankoros, without response. Then he ran a short distance away and turned back, helplessly, to watch.

The grave of Rannon's son exploded like an enormous fungus puffball, spewing stones, soil, and a white powder like an unseasonable snow. Whatever living things this powder touched, grass, trees, shrubs, died instantly, crumbling into ash.

And, as if some unheard voice warned them of the danger, birds from all over the island rose until the sky was black with them and their wings thundered. But the white dust rose also, a silent whirlwind, and touched the birds. They fell into the sea, spread upon it as a stain, and were gone.

"So Rannon! This is your vengeance!" Theremderis shouted. "It is worthy of you." And to himself he sobbed, "It is worthy of us all."

The sea crashed against the Black Cliffs like thunder. Theremderis felt the ground beneath his feet shake. A cold, harsh wind blew out of the north, whistling out of a grey, darkening sky, driving the dust in the direction of the castle.

The wind was the breath of Rannon himself, and the crashing his laughter.

The wizard's eyes burned. His throat felt dry, rough. The stuff was all around him. He ran. It followed like a living thing. His legs were tired, heavy. But his magic could shield him for a little while. He spoke words of protection, and closed off the air around himself, so that the dust could not touch him. For a little while.

He watched the dust pour out of the grave, swirling around dead trees even as they whitened and fell. The great boughs made no sound when they hit the ground, instead bursting into clouds of powder. Still the wind carried the white dust, spreading it like smoke.

Theremderis knew that this was something never before seen on Earth, the very essence of Rannon's power. It was the putrescent flesh of the death god's only son, corrupt beyond all comprehension, wholly inimical to life.

A herd of sheep came running by, bleating in terror. One by one the animals stumbled, fell, and were still. Theremderis prodded the nearest with his cane. The tip passed right through without any resistance. The sheep was like a thing sculpted out of sand. Soon the wind erased it. Soon its substance joined the ever-spreading cloud.

There was no end to the white stuff. It poured out of the grave in impossible quantities.

Theremderis ran, gasping, his heart pounding, until he reached a tree yet untouched by the contagion. He called a sparrow down from the branches, spoke some words and a name, and held an eagle in his hand. With another word, the eagle grew ten times its original size, until its outstretched wings dwarfed the old man.

"Quickly. Bear me up."

The eagle flapped, took hold of his hair, and lifted him, just as the tree paled and cracked and fell over in a flurry of dust. He dropped his cane and hung there, dangling, reaching up with both hands to ease the weight on his hair. Away they flew toward the other end of the island, where the castle called the Phoenix Nest stood, where a light still burned in the window of a certain tower; while below him, the island swiftly died.

The white death washed over all like a tide, covering, smothering, until the land and sky were silent, and nothing moved in the towns or along the roads.

Theremderis urged the bird on, fearful that he would not reach the castle in time.

Then he was ahead of the death-wave for a little while again, and he saw people running helplessly across the fields, clogging the roads with carts and animals. For a while he could hear their shouts, their screams. Then the air was foul with the dust again, even high up where he was, and there was only silence below.

Fields were burning. Peasants had set their crops and the stubble of their harvests on fire in an attempt to stay the advance. Smoke and flame even seemed to hold it off for a few minutes, then the tide moved as before and nothing remained to burn. Those who fought the menace perished as quickly and as uselessly as those who fled. That was Rannon's way.

He reached the castle at last, and the eagle spread its wings out straight, gliding toward the walls. All was quiet below. Sentries stood as they always had.

The momentary calm made Theremderis strangely calm also. His fear left him as he realised that he was like a physician come to announce that a dying patient had, at last, succumbed. Everything was, at the end, completely inevitable. His own fate was in other hands. He could only announce and observe and perhaps understand.

The eagle circled about the Tower of Eagles and for an instant Theremderis saw denuded forests standing like crystals, like wild sculptures of snow, crashing into swirling clouds. The whole scene was utterly silent, remote like a dream of endless winter. At this distance it was even beautiful.

Then the eagle dropped below the walls and set him down in the courtyard at the base of the tower. And Zio Theremderis dismissed his servant, bidding it flee on its mighty wings. The eagle flew, and the castle pigeons rose fluttering after it.

Without a word, but with speed that denied his age, Theremderis climbed the spiralling staircase of worn stone. He threw open the trapdoor and entered the upper room — and stood aghast at what he saw.

The blackened, swollen corpse of the Lady Riacinera lay in the middle of the floor amid scattered candlesticks. There were worms in her face, but still Prince Evnos knelt over her and, as the old man watched, bent and kissed her split, purple lips.

The Prince fondled the corpse's stringy hair and spoke in a high, hysterical voice which often broke.

"This is what I have written for you." Haltingly, he began reciting lines from *The Celebration of Riacinera*. There was an intensity in his manner, an obliviousness to his surroundings and true circumstances that Theremderis knew as a sure sign of madness.

The wizard held back tears as he put his hand on the other's shoulder and said, "My boy, what are you doing now?"

"What am I *doing?* I am speaking to my beloved. Have you become deaf, old man?"

"I am not deaf, my Prince, but she is. She cannot hear you. Her soul never left Rannon's kingdom."

"What are you talking about? *Can't you see that I succeeded?* I raised her up. I brought her back. Nothing *you* could do stopped me. I did it without you. I'll never need your help again. For anything."

"Lord, you have accomplished nothing but the deaths of all your people. Even now they are dying."

"*Who* said you could come in here anyway? Who said you could listen to our private conversations? *Didn't I send you away?*"

"Your people —"

"What do I care about my people? Go. Save them if you like. You have my permission. I have more important things to do, myself. The Lady Riacinera is with child. I must attend to her here."

"Come away now." Theremderis tugged at the Prince's shoulder. The other cursed vilely and glared up at him. Theremderis looked into that face and saw a hostile stranger, an enemy he had never met before, yet feared. The surpreme irony was that this monster had been created out of love and devotion and courage and little else.

"You!" the Prince screamed, leaping to his feet. "You did nothing to help me!"

"Please. Come away with me now. Leave this tower. It is a tomb, a stinking, open grave and nothing more. Leave your vain sorceries and —"

"Vain?" The Prince cocked his head weirdly to one side. He regarded Theremderis as he might a startlingly grotesque insect. His movements were sharp, abrupt. "You call them vain? After what I have done? You *dare?*"

Theremderis tried to be calm and firm. "You have done nothing. You are blind to the truth, yet that thing on the floor is only a corpse. It has no life. I, Zio Theremderis, your teacher, tell you this. But I can only beg you to believe me."

The young man ran a short distance, turned, and pointed, speaking in a distracted whisper as if to himself alone.

"You — *I know you.* I have known you all my life. You are my enemy. Whatever I wanted you took from me. You always refused to tell me what I wanted to know. You took my beloved from me once, and now you want to take her again. Yes, yes. That's it."

"That is not it," said Theremderis. His self-control was at an end. He wept openly. "No, not at all."

"Yes! Yes it is!" Evnos shrieked. Veins stood out on his forehead. He looked quickly from side to side, like a trapped animal. When he saw the dagger Theremderis wore on his belt — a ceremonial

dagger which the old man had worn for years — the expression on his face shifted from fear to amazement to something like fear. "Yes. That *is* it!"

Theremderis took a step toward him, extending his hand, and the Prince let out an almost womanish shriek. Before the wizard could react, Dran was out of its scabbard —

Dran was out, the Prince shrieked, and the sword passed right through the wizard's neck. Theremderis made a sound like a cough and his head spun through the air in a shower of blood, the look on his face one of utter astonishment.

The body fell backwards onto the floor, blood pouring from the open neck, the arms thrashing for an instant, then lying still.

"I told you to leave me! I told you I didn't want you around anymore. I told you that much. I did. I told you."

The rage passed, and the Prince stood quietly for a minute, breathing hard. He felt sick and weak.

Then he put the head and the body into the leather sack, tied the sack shut, and turned his attention once more to Riacinera.

A stray thought came to him, the prophecy of the Dwarf king: *Many heads shall this sword cut off, but the last shall be the head of wisdom.*

"The head of wisdom," Evnos mused. The shock of the killing had brought him halfway back to sanity, but only halfway. He trembled with horror and revulsion at something, but he could not find the memory. Something had been torn from him, ripped from his life, leaving a gaping wound behind — but he didn't know what. Everything was so confused, so tangled. The feeling was there, the pain, but the understanding was not.

Some catastrophe was happening to all of Iankoros. That much he remembered. He went to the window, looked out, and saw the front of a white cloud rushing toward him, hugging the ground like a tide of ash. The air was thick with white powder. Down below, guards on the walls ran, choked, fell.

The white stuff poured over the walls, into the castle itself. Somehow Prince Evnos knew what to do.

He bolted the windows and the trapdoor, sealing them with the blood of Theremderis, tracing with his finger the signs of Yoth and Caran Ctho and the countersign of Rannon.

Then he gazed sadly at the still form of Riacinera and said "Goodbye" very softly. He could not even weep. He was beyond all that now, his spirit too exhausted. As a hint of the truth filtered into his mind, there was only surrender. He knew that his task had been an impossible one.

He took up the herbs and ashes again, righted the candlesticks, and sat down with the *Book of Life* open on the floor in front of him. He spoke the words of life once more, but to a different purpose.

He sought only to save his child. This much he could do. The Death Lord could not claim one who had not yet lived.

Riacinera's womb began to swell visibly.

He gave the baby a name, a secret name neither male nor female, and with that name he held power over the child. With that name he summoned it forth, slowly, out of *unlife*. Hours passed. For a while, messengers came and pounded on the trapdoor, screaming words he could not make out. Then they were gone. The wind buffetted the tower, seeking an entrance, finding none. Toward evening the corpse's womb burst into tatters of blue-grey flesh, and Evnos lifted a living infant out of the remains.

It was a girl.

"Well, my heir shall be a princess then," he said. He sang a brief song of joy, the traditional celebration of a live birth, and gave the infant another name. Each line of his song rhymed with that new name: Amadel, meaning "flower of my flower."

When the sun again looked down on Iankoros, the island was a desolate table of stone rising from the sea. All life had been erased, save that which was sealed in the top of the Tower of Eagles. The halls of the Phoenix Nest were silent. The castle remained like a ship becalmed on a snowy ocean. Here and there, along the roads, a cart stuck out of the piled whiteness, empty and abandoned. The houses still stood, doors and windows gaping, silence within. Somehow the dust only destroyed living wood, not that cut and shaped by man. The rooftops remained above the drifts. But no trees survived. The hilltops were completely bare where the wind had blown away the white powder, naked rock and nothing more.

Weeks passed. Sailors came to Iankoros and turned away. They spoke of it by a new name, the White Isle, the place of death, and did not drop anchor there.

The changing seasons brought rain, and with the rain, friendly winds. Gradually the contagion was washed into the sea, and dead fish covered the shoreline of the mainland of Amyrthel for hundreds of miles. Again, in many lands, the name of Iankoros was cursed.

In the end, only the stones were left, and the dead soil where nothing would ever grow again. The sea cleansed itself, and gulls returned to the cliffs. But that was all. The Isle of the Phoenix was not reborn.

When he deemed it safe to do so, Prince Evnos opened his shutters, heaved the body of Zio Theremderis down into the courtyard below, and closed the shutters again.

In that instant, the baby beheld sunlight for the first time, and cried.

9 A Midnight Conversation

AS THE HOURS came and went in their steady pace, as the days were born and died beneath the sun and the clear evening sky, the Prince felt his madness retreat a little. Still it weighed on him heavily. He understood what he had done, what had happened. The horror of the situation remained. He was like one dazed with a wound, before the real pain begins. His future disintegration was clearer to him than any prophecy ever could be, a thing inevitable, yet to be resisted with grace and valor for all the ending would be the same. Perhaps he could gain a little time. He could not hope for more than that.

Therefore he occupied himself with tasks. It was safe to go out now. After many months, air was pure. The poison was gone from the land, as if the white powder had been recalled by Rannon as soon as the need for it had passed.

Evnos busied himself. He descended the winding stairs of the tower slowly, holding the baby in his arms. On those steps and on the floor below were scattered cloaks, helmets, swords, shields, trousers, tunics — reminders of messengers who had knocked on the trapdoor but were not answered. Not even their bones remained. The tower seemed like an ancient tomb, dust-filled, dry, but washed clean with years.

Outside in the courtyard one body did remain, that of Theremderis, which had been deposited after the infection had departed. The wizard's corpse was still in the sack, but the end had burst open and the head had rolled out. It lay facing the doorway as Evnos emerged, eyes rolled up till only the whites showed, bloodstained hair and beard ruffling slightly in the gentle breeze.

The Prince stopped. He stared, yet felt no revulsion at the sight, no dread of his guilt. There was only dull remorse. His emotions were purged from him, and he remembered them but dimly, as an old eunuch remembers his manhood when he daydreams.

"So, teacher," he said, "you are still here, to haunt me I suppose. It is only fitting."

There was not even sadness in his voice.

He gazed for awhile into the empty face, then walked on to the feasting hall where he had first glimpsed the shy daughter of the foreign king. The place was a ruin, tables smashed, the high throne overturned by someone in a final spasm of panic or rage. Heaps of clothing lay about, but the place was clean, dark and still.

At last he came to the nursery where he himself had once lain. It had been a pleasant room once, with sunlight shining through wide windows making the bright murals brighter still. Now it was faded and filled with dust.

He set the child down carefully in a cradle, then opened the shutters. They creaked, not having been opened in many years. This was a special room for the rearing of princes, used only by heirs to the royal house.

Then he realized he had just laid his child down in dust. He picked her up again and shook out the tiny mattress that lined the crib. It was still soiled, so he gave a command, "Be cleansed," and it was. He replaced it and laid the infant Amadel upon it. He spoke again, summoning mindless spirits out of the air, forming them into chambermaids armed with feather brushes. They set to work with frantic haste, ridding the room of all taint within minutes. When they were done, they all stood in a line before the Prince in the middle of the room, bowed once, and vanished into the air from which they had been called. Only his will had held them to their shapes. When his will relaxed, they were gone.

The Prince laughed lightly and said to the baby, "What an inspiration you are. If I'd bothered to do that before, the whole island would have been spotless."

He walked over the window and looked down on the brown, bare hills and the blue sea beyond.

"You shall remain here a while," he said, "as I did once, and I hope you will come to love this room as I did when I was small."

He reached out over the sill, straining, and took up a handful of earth from a gutter. He spat on it and formed it in his palm into the rough shape of a human figure, then recited a formula. The dirt

72

grew heavy. He let it drop, and before it touched the floor a middle-aged woman stood before him, completely motionless, her face without expression.

"Be awakened," he said, snapping his fingers in front of her eyes. "Care for my daughter."

Thus Amadel was reared by a nursemaid who dissolved into a pile of dust each night when the Prince slept, then reformed when he awoke in the morning. Her breasts gave no milk, so Evnos reached out with his magic far beyond the sea and robbed cows. Farmers cursed and blamed the shortage on snakes and witches. Evnos laughed. It was certainly the most humble task ever performed by an adept of the greater mysteries, but it was necessary. The nursemaid fed Amadel from a bottle. The Prince fed himself by magic also, sending his spirits forth to draw fish from the sea, or even to snatch bread and meat and wine from tables in other lands.

He staffed the palace with such spirits, called up one by one whenever some need occurred to him. They were only air, without personality or even gender unless he gave it to them, too insubstantial to lift solid objects unless he exerted himself additionally, and wont to vanish for good if he forgot about them for very long. When the nursemaid didn't return one morning a few years later, it was no great loss. After that the child was tended by the same airy creatures that maintained everything else.

Prince Evnos remained in deep melancholy, spending his time poring over old books in search of answers he could never find. He tried to amuse himself with poetry, but he had no patience with that of others and he could not bring himself to write his own. *The Celebration of Riacinera* was abandoned unfinished. Once he got the manuscript out, looked it over, sighed, and went to burn it in a fireplace before he realized what he was doing and recoiled in horror. This was the strongest emotion he had felt since . . . the blank time, which his mind hid from him. The sensation troubled him. He locked the manuscript away in a casket and never looked at it again.

His other verses he barely recognized. They were the work of some stranger, the inhabitant of a bright and furious world, an ancient epoch recalled only in dreams.

The future obsessed him. He tried to concentrate his thoughts on the void of the universe, where there was no life and consequently no death, neither Earth nor gods nor Rannon. This was the discipline of Hanoleth the Unspeaking, who had written a description of it for his disciples centuries before. But the Prince could not bring himself to follow the Unspeaking Way. His concentration broke. His meditation always drifted back to his own predicament, and to his daughter, and vague memories of Iankoros as it had once been. He was even tempted to brew a draught of forgetfulness and cleanse his mind completely, but he knew better. The peace he would achieve that way would be false. He would only come to his final confrontation with Rannon in blind ignorance. That would not serve him.

Still he could not actually *see* the future. There were no prophets left in the world, he knew, and there had been none since the battle of the Plain of Leboladen at the beginning of time, when the gods had fled from Rannon and mankind's power against death had been broken. Once the gods were gone, the future was closed to human eyes. Now there were only tricksters who spoke portentous vagueness for a penny. But there were no true prophets.

Therefore Evnos turned to the spirits for aid, to the travelling demons of the outer spaces. He studied the motions of the stars for months to find an auspicious night, and when one came, he was ready.

It was in the winter of Amadel's fourth year. The Prince made sure, on that night especially, that the child was kept occupied by the spirits he had summoned, protected, and locked in a room far away from the Tower of Eagles. When all was ready, and Evnos saw his daughter sitting with her ghostly storytellers and magicians, he sealed off her chamber with magic, then hurried to the top of his own great tower and turned his hands to the task they already knew well.

Once more he dipped a finger into ash paste and traced a circle on the floor, and within it a star, a triangle, and a square, following the faded patterns that still remained. The act seemed like something out of ancestral memory, recalled now from the actions of another performed ages ago. It was like walking along a familiar path without thinking where he was going.

He wrote in all the names that needed to be written, then lit the incense burners and torches. Some rare powders were not to be had, so he made substitutions. At last he bolted the door and opened a single window, letting the shutters swing wide.

When midnight came, he uncurled a roll of parchment, a list he had painstakingly compiled over the years from experiments, and from Theremderis's notes. It was far inferior to the Scroll of Summoning, but it contained a few dozen names and binding words and would have to do.

Again, in the brightly lit room, with the window open to the darkness, he called out names and reached with his mind and with outstretched arms into the abyss beyond the world. He felt the familiar cold, so intense that it burned through his whole body, and then a tug when he caught hold of his quarry.

Frigid wind blew in through the window, scattering papers about, making the torch flames sputter. Evnos stood still in the center of the circle, remembering each of his former mistakes, careful to avoid

74

any repetition. He rolled up the list and put it in an inner pocket, then waited for the spirit to arrive.

And the spirit came, and by some accident or unknown design it was a creature he knew. It was Gladziri.

Firmly, calmly, he spoke the familiar word to bind the spirit in place, and the demon lingered before him, motionless, invisible. The wind ceased, and he seemed to be alone. But he knew better. He *felt* the presence of the entity, and its power made him tremble, even now after all he had been through. He looked about. Nothing stirred in the room. Incense rose slowly, curling beneath the ceiling.

Suddenly a mouse scurried from beneath a bookshelf.

"Stop!" He called out the secret name of the mouse tribe. The mouse kept on going.

"Gladziri! Stop!" He spoke another binding word, and the mouse vanished into the air in the middle of the floor. Once more the wind whirled around the room. Dust rose. Evnos felt a brief, hot blast on his face, as if a furnace door had been opened and closed. Then came a rustling, like someone walking on fallen leaves. He sensed the mind of the demon as clearly as he had that time before, during his previous conjuring, but now there was a change. The hatred was not absolute. The contempt, if anything, had increased, but there was another emotion. Was it mirth?

Gladziri spoke in a soft voice, almost like that of a young girl, but toneless and inhuman.

"Very good, little man. You saw my ruse and countered it. I would almost suspect you of intelligence, were such refinements ever found among your kind. Alas, they are not. Still, you are improving. I ask you for mercy this time. You give me so little peace. You tire me. Was it not the other night you called me and made me work so hard?"

"It was six years ago."

"It is all the same to me. A night, a year, a millennium, are all the same. We higher beings are not bound by time the way certain vermin are."

"I sadly conclude that you are of no use to me then," said Evnos, "since I had wanted to question you about time. By your own admission you are ignorant of the subject. I had thought you wise, but am disappointed."

The demon laughed, its voice now like rolling thunder.

"Ha! You try to wound my pride! Again, well done. I had underestimated you. Not by much, for you are still ridiculously unlearned, but by a little bit. Of course I know about time. We who have true intelligence look on many things which are hidden from the eyes of worldling-lice."

Evnos remained unmoved by the taunts. He had expected as much.

It was part of the ritual. At the same time, he was beginning to enjoy the exercise of his own wit, but he remained cautious, lest the creature distract him with the verbal give-and-take.

"Let us get on with our business," he said. "I wish to know the future. You must show me the days ahead."

Gladziri's voice changed again, becoming high and shrill like that of a scolding harridan. "Oh, tush, tush. Now it is my turn to be disappointed. Why do you bother me with trifles? Why not go to one of your human witches, hire her to pickle a raven's brain and read the future out of the dirt around your arse? That is the way they do it these days, is it not?"

"It seems, O Gladziri, that I was right about you the first time," the Prince said. "You are truly stupid, for anyone who is intelligent or learned knows that such methods are false, and serve only to beguile the simple-minded."

"Ah! *So you have become learned then?* Some god has picked his nose and the result is a scholar. Marvel of marvels!"

Evnos spoke another word, binding Gladziri tighter, yanking as a houndmaster pulls on a leash.

The demon squealed. *"Behold your future!"*

And Prince Evnos saw. The smoke of the incense burners and torches gathered into one place, flowing together like water. Long, pale hands appeared in the middle of the cloud, holding a black disk the size of a shield.

"Look here, little man —"

The disk was a kind of window, through which Evnos gazed down into a vast abyss. At first he made out only suggestions of shapes, then a sea of clouds, and then the viewpoint dropped through the clouds to reveal stark, barren hillsides and a teeming land the Prince knew all to well.

It was the Underearth. The vision lasted for but a second before the eye of the disk descended again, down a long shaft of stone like a chimney. The window was dark for several minutes.

At last, in the darkness, two yellow eyes opened. Something huge stirred and shifted back from the window. Its face became visible, an enormous, leathery mask glistening with moisture around two cavernous nostrils. Two dirty white tusks protruded from fleshy jowls.

"Rannon! Is it you?"

"It is I, Evnos of Iankoros. Indeed, it is I." The voice was muted but vast, like the first stirrings of an earthquake. Evnos was too overwhelmed by the sight and the voice to say anything. The death god stared at him and laughed. "You wonder how I know who you are. I shall impart to you a great secret then, Prince Evnos of Iankoros, whose secret soul-name is *Drothmond*, and that is that I know the names of all men living, dead, and yet to be born. That is how I own them. They are my chattel, my larder. I know your daughter Amadel, whose true name is Zylogaena, and I have reserved a place of honor for her in my kingdom, as I have for you. When you sent the wizard Theremderis to me, I welcomed him as an old friend and escorted him to his new abode. *He boils in a pot of lead, and the fire is fueled with books.* Would you like to see him, Prince Evnos of Iankoros?"

"No! Please! I beg —"

"When you come to my land to dwell here forever, then you shall see. You shall reside near him. Come now, if you like . . ."

"I am not ready," said Prince Evnos softly.

"But I am."

"I escaped you once." Evnos's voice began to break under the strain. His words came out in a hoarse whisper. He was afraid he would faint.

"You only served my purpose," said Rannon. "When you returned to your own kingdom, you handed over all your subjects to me. Now Iankoros is *my* domain and I rule there. I shall take you too when I want to. But for the great boon you have granted me, I have condescended to let you live a while longer. I have rewarded my son, too, for his part in the enterprise. He performed his mission well. I am building a new body for him, which he will find more . . . pleasing . . . than the old one."

"You lie. All of this is a lie." Evnos was babbling. He did not believe what he was saying. "I *command* you. I have summoned you. I command you to tell me what I want to know."

"What, then, do you wish to know?" asked the thing in the darkness.

"My future."

"Idiot, *I* am your future. I am Amadel's future and Theremderis's future and Riacinera's future, and yours, unto the ending of time."

"Do not speak the name of my beloved! You defile her!"

"I can speak the names of my slaves whenever I please, Prince Evnos, who is truly Drothmond. Yes, you did love Riacinera, whatever that means. Is this not so? Would it please you to look on her face again? I can accomplish that much for you."

"How? What do you want?"

"Nothing much. *You.* You are nothing much. You shall be subject to my every whim, as she is now. Remember, O Prince, that *I still have the Lady Riacinera in my own country.*"

"Lies! Lies!" Evnos sobbed. But he knew they were not lies.

The god laughed and the tower shook. The Prince fell to his knees in the middle of the circle, covering his face with his hands. When at last he dared to look up, the window was gone and Gladziri had reverted to invisibility.

"Such is your future, little man. Why did you ever doubt it? All men can see their future quite easily, in the faces of the dead. But they choose not to. They please themselves with pretty dreams, and so, blindly, they walk down tangled paths, all of which lead to Rannon. There is no other possible ending."

"Then life is a meaningless horror," said the Prince.

"I cannot agree." Gladziri chuckled. "The comedy of your existence sometimes amuses those above you. For that reason it is allowed to continue."

"No more! I shall destroy myself, and that will end your games."

"You'll . . . kill yourself? And drop right into Rannon's lap?"

"I shall find another way. I shall kill my soul too, so there is nothing left."

"There was once a man called Hinaris," mused the demon, "who alone of all born of women managed to evade Rannon. He blew his soul out like a candle flame, so they say."

"Leave me, creature," said Evnos, "while I seek the wisdom of Hinaris." He spoke the word of Gladziri's unbinding, then the command of banishment.

Yet the demon remained. It rustled back and forth as if it were pacing, and wheezed.

"Begone!" the Prince cried.

"No, I shall not leave just yet," the demon said. A visible form coalesced out of the air: a serpent with thick arms and powerful legs rearing up until it had to bend its neck and stoop beneath the ceiling. A clawed foot smeared the line of ash-paste on the floor and Gladziri entered the circle.

Evnos stood, frozen in helpless horror. "What is this? Leave me! I command you by your secret name, by the names of my mighty ancestors —"

"All of whom," the demon hissed, "are quite, quite *dead*."

"I command —"

"You command nothing, Prince of Nothing, ruler of the island of mud and ruined houses. Your power is as dead as your domain. Your own selfish pride killed it. Your folly killed it. You can work no great magic now. You cannot conjure. You did not summon me, little one. I came of my own will. It is my part in the comedy, which I gladly fulfill. I am beginning to appreciate the sport Rannon finds in your kind. I could have scattered your limbs across the world if I had wanted to, at any time during this amusing encounter, but, no, I *chose* not to. Perhaps I am learning mercy, little man? Do you think so?"

The demon towered over Evnos, who backed out of the circle,

colliding with a shelf. Books and bottles rained down. Gladziri leaned down and brushed the shelf aside, ripping it from the wall with a single swipe of a huge claw. The Prince ducked to the floor, then remained there, motionless, in complete surrender.

"I tire of this," said Gladziri. "I leave you now with a reminder of my esteem. Little man, do you know what it is, the mark of Gladziri?"

Evnos looked up. He could not answer. There were no words. Suddenly the demon's searingly bright tongue lashed out, and the Prince's face was burning as if he had been struck by a molten hammer. He raised his hands to protect his eyes, and his hands were burning, hissing, smoke rising from them. He screamed and fell back down. The room seemed filled with fire for an instant, and then was totally dark. He clawed at his face, at his clothing, until he huddled in the middle of the floor, in the blind darkness, half naked, vomiting from the hideous fumes that filled the room, sobbing all the while, *"Why? Why should I go on? I cannot live. I cannot even die —"*

And at that moment, against as if by accident or some mysterious design, he heard the far-away music of the ghostly musicians as they played for Amadel, and he heard her voice shrieking with laughter at some jest, and he said softly, "I am answered," and lost consciousness.

A while later he awoke, still in darkness. He groped to the window, leaned out, and saw, with amazed disbelief, the first glow of dawn in the east. He raised his hand before his eyes and wept for joy, for the slight reprieve of not being blinded. He saw that his hand was blackened and shrivelled, and he felt the pain of the burned flesh, which was already swelling, but for that moment it seemed enough that he was still alive, and could see, and somewhere, in another part of the castle, Amadel was safe from harm.

"This terror is like a passing dream, and yet it is not a dream, for it has not passed, and I have awakened into it."

He might have been quoting something. He wasn't sure. Again he wept.

10 The Flower of Jankoros

TIME SPOKE to the island in signs and in seasons. Spring followed a white winter, and summer came. Rain washed the naked land, and the wind blew warm, then cold as autumn neared, then bitter, then warm again; constellations wheeled in the sky. Prince Evnos watched the passing months with a vague feeling of sorrow. He saw the deep furrows trace themselves across the slopes of the hills, like wrinkles on an old woman's face. He saw debris washed up on the beaches after storms. Once in a while there was a sail far off, which would grow larger for a while, then diminish to nothing. On clear days he could make out the flat blue-gray line of the mainland, like the edge of another, unattainable world.

Amadel was his chief joy. She could draw him out of his melancholy for a little while, make him smile, laugh, and live, for a few minutes at least, as a human being. Otherwise he was an automaton.

She was a large, beautiful child with a wild riot of curly hair, like her father's when he was younger. She had her mother's face, and eyes green as the ocean depths. Her disposition, as Evnos once told her, was that of a little monkey, but a monkey filled with charm and kindness and occasionally even good manners; the kind of monkey who would one day be a great lady, once she grew up and her tail fell off.

The little girl was happy in those days. She had been born into a castle filled with spirits, in the midst of a barren land. She knew

80

nothing else. To her, there were two kinds of people in the world, those through whom she could pass her hand, who were sometimes nearly transparent if the light shone through them just so; and her father, who was solid like herself.

Her father was the source of all wisdom and marvels. The universe revolved around him. For a time she had truly believed that he had created the world, spreading out the sea like a blue cloth, placing the sun and moon carefully in the sky.

Once she pointed out a window at the dun-colored hills and asked, "What is that?"

"That is my realm," Evnos answered.

"And what's beyond it?"

"The sea."

"I think the sea is more beautiful than the land," said Amadel. "What comes after the sea?"

The Prince paused, stroking his beard, as if thinking deeply.

"A most profound question, young lady. Have you ever seen anything beyond the sea?"

"Sometimes. When I climb up in the towers and look out on a bright day, there is something far away, at the edge of the sea, like a cloud that doesn't move."

"It is land. Just more land. You have enough here, don't you?"

"I like the water better."

Amadel did prefer the ocean. She played by its shore whenever she could, leading her trains of ghostly servants. In the bright sunlight, on the beach, they were nearly invisible. She could tell where they were only by the way they stirred up the land into little whirlwinds as they walked.

She collected shells and weeds and other strange things left for her by the waves. The water itself was a wonder. She waded out into it and saw that it was filled with living things, fish, crabs, wriggling eels. Birds flew the water and dipped into it. Some rested on it, drifting up and down like foam. Endlessly, the waves rose and fell, whispering with their own muted, mysterious voices. All this was much more interesting than the empty, silent land.

The greatest mystery of all was the passage of ships at great distances. She knew from tales what they were, and she imagined them filled with spirits, like her servants. She was certain that she and her father were the only solid, real people in the world.

The ships drifted like clouds, sometimes their sails growing tall and broad, before they shrank again to mere specks on the horizon. She called out to them sometimes, but they went on their way and did not answer. The ships reminded her of the high-flying birds, so far away that they were beyond the reach of all things.

This, to Amadel, was merely the way of things, yet she wondered what it would be like to touch one of those ships, or, more incredibly, to stand upon its deck. Would she fall right through it, into the water? Or would it be half-solid, like a drifting mass of seaweed? There was always a certain confusion in her mind between substantial and ghostly things, between those that remained always and those that were gone when no one paid attention to them anymore.

Once Amadel was afraid that *she* would fade away in her sleep if no one were there, and so, for several nights she refused to go to bed unless the bemused Evnos stood over her, reassuring her again and again that he would always remember her, and that would be enough. When he tired of this, he gave his shape to a spirit, which stood there all night lest she awaken and find herself alone. In the morning, she did find herself alone, for the spirit would dissolve in the glow of morning, but Amadel was not afraid of vanishing in the daylight.

Each day he would explain to her, "I have no magic over you. I just watched. For a while I fell asleep, and didn't watch. But you're still here. Isn't that strange?"

Then he would laugh, and she would laugh also. The fear diminished, until it ceased to trouble her. Real people, she learned, remained in existence no matter what. Only she and her father were real then, unless one counted the gulls and the creatures of the sea.

Amadel continued to ask questions. Evnos answered them as best he could. One day he walked with her in the courtyard below the Tower of Eagles, and they came to something round and white and hollow. Amadel stooped to touch the thing, but paused. She had seen this object many times before, but had never asked what it was. It seemed somehow unpleasant. Scattered around were other white things, and scraps of an old sack.

"Father, what are these?"

"Only bones, child."

"Whose? Don't bones come from people?"

"I don't know. Perhaps they are the bones of Iankoros itself."

This puzzled Amadel. She regarded the bones.

"How did they get here?"

"Perhaps they fell out of the sky," said Prince Evnos. There was a trace of irritation in his voice. "Perhaps they've been here forever."

"Which was it?"

"How should I know? I didn't see them fall, and I haven't been here forever."

"You mean you *don't know?*"

"No. Yes. That's it. I don't know. Nobody knows everything." He took her by the hand and dragged her away. He wouldn't answer any more questions that day.

The great dilemma of his position was obvious enough to Evnos. His daughter would continue to ask questions. As she grew older, the probing would grow ever more incisive. All the things he had hidden from her, she would discover eventually. He could only gain time by his deceits, holding off the inevitable. He had not even lied to her in any consistent way, but had only made up excuses as each situation arose. Once he had considered inventing a whole tapestry of lies, and bringing her up in a world of total illusion, but he could not force himself to do it. Besides, he was busy with his researches. He couldn't concentrate on other matters, even lies. So he had hesitated until it was too late. She knew too much already. Her mind was growing fast.

Before long, he knew, she would be asking about her mother. He had so far managed to avoid the subject and explain away occasional slips of the tongue. But the contradictions would soon become a ludicrous tangle. Her attendants read stories to her. She had already asked why people in stories always had two parents, while she had only one. Those were only stories, he told her.

It hurt him to lie to her, but he kept on doing it. He realized that he was afraid of losing her. He was afraid she would come to hate him.

In the meantime, he tried to keep her amused.

Therefore he conjured a playmate for her, a cloud drawn from the sky, filled with earth and water, given shape and duration by his magic. He sent it drifting toward her, and when its feet touched the ground it became a solid thing, its footsteps echoing as it walked along a narrow passage between the great hall of the castle and the outer wall.

Evnos watched the whole scene through a mirrored glass he held in his hand.

He saw — and he heard — Amadel gasp with delight and astonishment. She stood in the open yard behind the armory, where in the old times soldiers had practiced with their weapons. Now it was a bare patch of ground. Amadel had never known it as anything else.

But suddenly golden and luminescent blue flowers rose up out of the earth, uncurled, and stood swaying all around her. They climbed the walls, growing out of the very stones.

She picked one, found it solid and real, and gasped. It did not vanish like smoke, the way most illusions did. She waded through them gingerly, then let out a yelp when a boy sat up in the midst of them and said, "Do you like my flowers?"

This was the companion Evnos had sent to her.

"They're beautiful!" said Amadel.

"Pick one."

"I already did."

"Pick more!"

Before long she held a bouquet, glimmering in the sunlight. She reached out to touch him, and drew back startled when she could not pass her hand through him.

"Who are you?"

The playmate spoke, but no words came. Evnos, watching, realized that he had not given the creature any name. He shrugged, drew the glass nearer to his mouth, and whispered, "Cloud."

"I am called Cloud," the boy said.

"But —?" Amadel stared up at the sky, where white clouds drifted.

"My father is the sky," the boy said. "All the clouds are his children. When I came down to visit you, I made myself look like this."

"You came down to visit me?"

"Yes. To play with you. I can do magic."

She didn't seem very impressed. "*My* father does magic too."

"Watch!" The boy clapped his hands — truly clapped them, as no spirit she had ever known could — and each of the blue flowers brought forth a new stem from the center of its blossom. The stems grew as she watched, their tips bulging, at last opening into fire-bursts of red blossoms. The topheavy plants bent toward the ground.

"How do you like that?"

"Can you do more?"

"Yes!" Once more he clapped his hands, and the red flowers sprouted orange ones, from which came white, pink, gold, and green all in turn. The long chains of them covered the walls now, and lay on the ground in curling heaps.

"What else can you do?"

"Sing songs. Would you like a song?"

"Yes," said Amadel. "A merry one."

"A merry song indeed," the boy said, and he sang in a high, sweet voice:

"A wizard there was who lived in the air,
Yes he lived up in the air!
And he had a wife, whose temper was rife —
She scared all the spirits up there!
Oh! She scared all the spirits up there!

"This wizard he hid himself under the ground.
Yes! He hid under the ground!
But alas! His dear wife, she also came down,

84

and chased him 'round and 'round.
Oh! She chased him 'round and round.

"The wizard he turned himself into a toad,
an ugly old horny old toad!
But his ugly old wife became a toad too —
'Oh! I'll never let go of you!
No! I'll never let go of you.' "

Evnos, holding the mirror, smiled. He remembered that song from his own childhood. His father's fool had sung it to him many times.

Amadel frowned.

"What is the matter?" asked Cloud. "Wasn't it merry enough?"

Evnos, watching, struck his forehead with his palm. "I'm the fool now," he said aloud, to himself.

"I'm the —" said the boy.

"What?"

"Didn't you like the song? Wasn't it merry enough?"

"It's fine. But I don't understand. What's a wife? Is she like . . . a mother? Why didn't they love each other? Was she wicked?"

Cloud shrugged. "I don't know. It's just a song."

Evnos paused. He had to think of something quickly, to distract Amadel quickly before more and more disturbing meanings came unraveled out of that simple, silly song. He whispered into the glass.

"Well!" said Cloud. "I shall have to come up with something better. In the meantime, look behind you."

She turned, and her mouth drew into a wide, soundless *O*. There before her, knee-deep in the flowers, was a creature half like a horse, half like a bird. It had a horse's legs and tail, but was covered with delicate white feathers. The long tapering neck ended in a bird's head. Its eyes were like polished black stones, its beak green, like carven, rounded jade.

The creature opened its huge wings and flapped, making a sound like a muffled thunderclap.

"This is Master Wind," said the boy. The creature neighed. "He likes you."

"I like him too," said Amadel shyly.

"Climb up on his back."

She tried, but it was too high. She slid away, grasping a handful of feathers.

"I'm sorry."

The bird-horse neighed again.

"He says it's all right. Come." The boy lifted her onto the creature's back, then mounted behind her. He placed one arm around her and with the other hand tightly clutched the feathers on the animal's neck.

"Up," Evnos whispered into the mirror.

"Up!" the boy shouted. "Up! Up!"

Master Wind galloped around the yard, kicking up flowers, flapping his wings, faster and faster. Then with a heaving leap he was in the air. His hooves sparked against the top of the armory roof. The great wings flapped, caught the air, flapped, climbing. The creature seemed to gallop through the very sky.

Amadel looked down. The towers and walls of the castle were tiny, shrinking, circling as she watched. Still Master Wind climbed, less furiously now, his wing-strokes long and graceful, like those of an enormous swan. The isle of Iankoros was a brown patch in a blue sea. Beyond it, to the west, the mainland of Amyrthel stretched green with its fields and forests.

Cold wind howled around them now. Amadel had to shout to be heard.

"Why is that land a different color?"

"Because it's not your country. It's different." The boy shouted too, his voice trailing off.

"What's it like?"

"What?"

"The other place. The green country."

"Just different."

"Can I go there someday?"

"Maybe. Look!"

She leaned forward and looked. Between the rise and fall of wings she saw the whole Earth spread out beneath her, the sun sinking in the west beyond the edge of the world. Iankoros was reduced to a mere speck, and all the lands seemed tiny, bounded by the enormous ocean. Only to the south was it different. There a vast continent stretched to the very rim, as brown and barren as her homeland.

"It is the Great Stone Waste," Cloud shouted. "No one ever goes there."

Now the shape of universe itself was clearly visible. To the south, beyond the waste and the world's edge, was only air. To the east, water poured past Elimdorath the Beautiful and the Last Isles, spraying into the abyss. To the north, where Rannon waited, were only ice and mist. And to the west, fire, where the sun set. Barely visible beyond all this, gleaming, then vanishing in the darkness, the scales of the Shōmar, the World-Serpent, slid slowly by.

Evnos had explained all this to Amadel before, pointed to a chart. She hadn't understood then. Now she seemed to think it wonderful beyond all description.

Still higher the winged steed soared. The Moon rose out of the east, and comets, like ships in the night, passed close by. Amadel — and Evnos, listening through the mirror — heard the ancient songs of the departed gods, which still echoed between the stars.

"Enough," the Prince said gently. "Return. Return."

"We have to go back," Cloud said. The air was thinner. His voice was like a distant whisper.

"Why?" said Amadel.

There was no answer. Master Wind began to descend. When he reached the lower sky, beneath the course of the sun, it was evening. The sky steadily darkened. The newly-risen Moon shone full, like a lantern against the purple heaven. The lands were hidden from view, and the sea was in shadow by the time the steed and riders neared the castle. The constellation of the Blind Archer stood guard over the western horizon, more distinct as the last sunlight faded.

Amadel stepped down from Master Wind's back, unsteady now that there was solid ground underfoot again. She stood in the bare yard by the armory. The flowers had vanished.

"I want to do it again," she said. "Can we? Soon?"

"Someday. Not soon," the Prince said into the mirror.

"I think so, but not right away."

"Why *not?*"

"There are so many other things to do."

"But I *want* to!" Amadel said, stamping her feet in frustration.

"Now, don't be like that. Look here!" Cloud pointed.

She turned, and as she did the flowers sprouted from the stones and mud once more, growing even as she watched, rising over the armory roof like a wave. Suddenly, they vanished as quickly and completely as a burst bubble.

Amadel turned back, looking for Cloud and Wind.

Both of them were gone. She was alone in the bare yard.

The Prince sighed, and placed the mirror gently face down on the top of his desk.

He hoped all this would be for the best. When he was not caught up completely in his own obsessive researches, he still had time to think of his daughter. He made plans for her. There was nothing else in his life.

She would always remember what she had seen this day. Right

now, her vision of the scheme of things was only a vivid wonder, like a dream. Understanding would come later. She had seen the world's four directions, the realms of water, ice, fire, and air beyond the rim, on which the four seasons and the four humours were attendant. Philosophers could only speculate on such things. Amadel had *seen*. She had seen the world-serpent and the ice-lands of Rannon.

It was his hope, his plan for her, that Amadel would remain always apart from the rest of humanity. The very opening of her eyes to the secrets of the universe would accomplish this purpose. She would be the sighted one among the blind, impatient with, uninterested in all the rest of her species, those who had not seen the wonders she took for granted.

That was his plan, that she should, in time, join him in the contemplation of the deepest mysteries. One day she would be a magician as great as he.

Opening Doors

WHEN AMADEL was eight, she asked to be taught to read. Evnos taught her. The Prince had feared this thing, delaying it as long as possible; but inevitably she tired of being read to, and when she saw him reading by himself, she often watched with obvious fascination, sensing the power of words.

So, when she came to him one day with a book in her hands, piping cheerfully, "Show me how to read this, Father," he could not refuse. Could he deny the wind? It was nothing he could prevent.

Still, he was afraid. Her mind was active. She learned so much so fast. One day she would be a woman, with full understanding. She would see through his half-truths. She would know what he had done. In the end, how would she regard him, with pity or with horror?

When the request was made, he stood silently. The child tugged on his sleeve.

"I'm very smart," she said. "I learned the songs you taught me. I can learn this too."

"Yes, you certainly can," he said.

He took the book from her. It was a volume he had read very carefully once, very long ago; a massive thing bound in hide, studded with jewels, and locked with a silver hasp. He carried the book to a table, set it down, and pulled up a chair. Amadel dragged a stool over and sat beside him.

Evnos ran his hands slowly over the book's cover, wiping off dust, feeling the familiar texture of the jeweled boards. As he did he remembered how another man had once sat with another child over this same volume, and how they struggled together over the magic of letters.

For an instant he seemed to see Theremderis, staring at him out of the book cover as if through a window, his beard streaming in the harsh wind. The old man was shouting something. Evnos couldn't quite make it out.

Then the Prince was merely in a daze. Something in his mind had rejected the vision. He sat there, staring at the brown hide of the book cover.

"Father?"

"Yes?" He was aware of the room around him again, and of Amadel beside him. He turned toward her and she smiled weakly, a little afraid. "I was just thinking," he said. "The book made me . . . remember. But don't worry. I'll teach you."

"I couldn't get the lock off," said Amadel.

"Well, let me look at it." The Prince turned the book and saw that the hasp was held shut by a tiny padlock no larger than a thumbnail. It puzzled him for a moment. Then he recalled who had put that lock there, how, and why.

It was only fitting that Amadel should have selected this particular book. Perhaps even the choice itself was part of the design of Galthamis the Crafty, who was said to have spent his entire life fashioning this single lock and book.

"How does it open?"

"A key must be turned three times."

"What key? Do you have it, Father?"

"No, little one. You do."

"But I don't!"

"You *are* the key, Daughter." He gazed intently into her face, and her eyes grew wide with confusion and something close to fear. He pointed to the keyhole and said, "Now go inside."

She was falling, dizzily, in complete darkness, but somehow her mind was numbed. Everything was remote, happening, it seemed, to someone else. She wasn't even afraid.

She came to rest with a bump, as if she had slipped off her stool. Still the darkness was absolute, and she found herself sitting on a cold, smooth floor that felt not like stone but like metal.

She stood up, shivering, the floor like ice through her thin slippers. She groped around for a wall or a door, but touched nothing.

"Hello! Hello!" Her voice echoed back in the stale air from great distances, suggesting a large hall or cavern. She tried to be brave, to deny any fear, but her heart beat faster and faster. When she stood still and held her breath, she could hear it. There was no other sound.

She was truly alone for the first time in her life. How could her father protect her here? Where was his magic now? Did he even know where she was?

She stretched out her hands again into the darkness, swinging her arms gently back and forth at shoulder level, all the while walking forward slowly, her knees buckling, afraid that at any moment she would fall down a flight of unseen stairs or into a hole. But she did not fall. After what felt like hours she came to a wall as cold and smooth as the floor, and she hugged the wall with relief, breathing heavily. Then she continued to walk, sliding her hand along the wall, careful not to lose it in the dark. The wall seemed to be curving gently, but she could not be sure. There was no point of reference.

Her eyes began to deceive her in the total absence of light. She saw spots like after-images, blue and red, pulsating as they drifted to one side or the other, then faded. It was as if she had closed her eyes and pressed her fingers against the lids, creating that sort of ghostly shape.

She put her hand to her face, to make sure that her eyes were indeed still open. They were, but she could not see her hand.

When she finally saw a light ahead, she thought it likewise unreal, but it did not drift or fade. Instead, it grew as she neared it, from a tiny point to a steady glow. When she was very close she could make out a lantern held by a bent figure in a hooded cloak.

"Hello! Help me! I'm lost!"

The lantern bearer turned, but did not speak. She still could not see his face.

"What place is this?" she asked. "Can you help me get out?"

The hooded one remained silent. She approached cautiously, observing as she did that he was a solid person and that the light did not shine through him as it would through a spirit.

"Father? Is that you?"

The lantern was held higher, a word whispered, and the light increased. Still she could discern no face beneath the hood, but she could tell that they were standing in a round chamber of gray metal. The ceiling was high, lost in the gloom. Evenly spaced around the room, four arched openings gaped like huge mouths. She had emerged from one of them.

"Who are you?" the stranger asked in a voice like a tolling bell. Most certainly it was not her father's voice.

"I am Amadel," she said defensively.

"Go that way." The other pointed to one of the openings.

She walked a few steps, reluctant to leave the light, and turned.

"Will you go with me?"

The light winked out and she was alone.

With desperate care, but uncertainly, she shuffled in what she hoped was a straight line, arms outstretched, until she once more touched a metal wall. She had reached a sharp corner, the entrance to one of the passages. She stood there for a moment, then went in, slowly and deliberately, trying not to think that it might be the wrong one. She was very close to panic now.

Her footsteps echoed in the empty silence, and the sound of them came back only after a long time. She continued on, one hand touching the wall, the floor burningly cold beneath her feet, and she wondered what this all meant. She remembered the book, the keyhole, and her father's strange words. She did not understand.

Finally, after what might have been hours or even days in the timeless dark, she banged into something hard without warning and hurt her nose. It was another wall. The echoes had been different for a while by then, returning quickly, sometimes seeming to have come from behind her.

She had reached the end of the tunnel and there was no door, no way out at all. She ran her hands over the entire surface, from the floor to as high as she could reach, then worked her way sideways until she came to yet another, the opposite side of the passage.

The tunnel was a dead end. She must have taken the wrong one, she told herself. She would have to go back and find the correct one. Again, panic rose in her. Why had the light-bearer vanished so quickly, before she had reached the proper opening?

All the way back she pondered this. She walked more quickly this time, along the same wall she had followed in, knowing, at least, that the way was safe. By the time she got to the opening her legs were tired and her feet numb with the cold.

The hooded one was there with his light.

"Hello! Help me again! I went the wrong way."

"Who are you?" Again the voice was booming and hollow.

"Why, I am Amadel."

The stranger pointed to the passage from which she had just emerged.

"That's the wrong way. It doesn't go anywhere."

"Who are you?"

"I am a princess, the Princess of Iankoros, the greatest princess in the world. Listen, you had better show me the way out right now or I'll —"

"Go that way." Again the man pointed, to a different tunnel this time.

"Hold the light till I get there, at least. This is my command. I'm a princess, you know."

The other said nothing, but accompanied her to the tunnel mouth, footsteps echoing loudly. Then the light winked out again, and once more she was alone.

"Hey! Where are you? Come back!"

She flailed her arms around through the cold, musty air. When she was sure he was not nearby, she entered the tunnel, groped her way to the side of it, and proceeded.

This tunnel seemed to go on much longer than the previous one had, and she grew weary. Her breath came in hoarse sobs, the bitterly cold air stabbing her lungs. She dared not stop, dared not rest, fearing anything that might creep upon her in the dark, or simply that she would freeze to death. She understood freezing. She had seen dead birds in the winter.

Her mind was a muddle. She tried to find some meaning in all that was happening, but it refused to make sense. One minute she had been in a familiar room with her father asking to be shown how to read a book, and then, this. Had a more powerful wizard snatched her away while he was distracted with opening the book? Was that *possible?* Could someone do that in her father's own castle?

No, she decided. It was not possible. That was not the explanation.

She wondered if this were what it meant to be dead.

She walked with her right hand brushing the wall. Then, perhaps because of the closeness of the air, or because of some instinct she could not define, she suddenly reached out with her left — and touched something solid, smooth, and cold. It was another wall. She followed them both with her outstretched hands, and after a while became aware that they were drawing closer together.

Then she felt something pressing down on her head, the ceiling, and she had to proceed bent over, as the tunnel narrowed even more. She was forced to crawl, and it seemed that the tunnel rose in a gradual slope, as if floor, walls, and ceiling were all converging on some distant point.

She wanted out. Blindly, desperately, like a trapped thing, she wanted out. The air was thick. She could hardly breathe. She felt the infinite weight of the walls and ceiling, pressing, crushing her. But still she continued, because she was a princess, and a princess should be brave, she told herself; burrowing like a mole in the iron earth, hoping that she might, just *might* come into the light and the warmth of the world again, if she were brave enough, strong enough.

The darkness throbbed like a living thing. She struggled for breath. Somehow, despite the cold, her body ran with sweat. When she could no longer crawl, she dropped to her belly and wriggled, her arms out in front, the passage too narrow now for her to bring them back. The walls and floor no longer met at right angles, but had fused together into a curve. The tunnel was a tube, constricting, about to be pinched off. Yet some intense, irrational urge drove her on, the urge to escape by some feat of struggle and fury, to break out of the darkness, into the light.

It was only when she gasped for air and found there was no room to expand her chest that she realized the full horror of her situation. The tunnel pressed tight against her hips and shoulders. Her arms were pressed over her ears. Her pulse thundered.

She couldn't scream. She let out a long, whining, sobbing moan, and tried to back out of the tunnel.

She was stuck. She could not move her arms down below her shoulders to push. Her elbows hit the walls. There was only smooth metal for her feet to kick against.

"Father, help me. Help me . . ."

She sobbed, tears running down her face, while her whole body trembled uncontrollably, from terror, from the cold.

After a while she managed to wriggle backwards a little, pushing the metal away with her fingers. It seemed like hours before she had enough room to move her arms. Still the endless weight of the tunnel pressed on her, and she felt herself suffocating. She breathed desperately, hissing through her teeth.

She began to crawl backwards, screaming wildly, incoherently, without even syllables, and her cries gurgled back to her in mocking echoes.

She continued backwards, ever backwards, elbows and knees banging painfully, until she found she could turn around. Then she crawled faster, scurrying into the darkness ahead. At last she came to the end of the tunnel, stumbling, crawling, running a little ways, then crawling again, screaming for her father.

He did not come, but the lantern bearer was waiting for her.

She grasped him, clinging to him as if he were a post and she drowning, sobbing over and over, "Father, Father, help me."

And the other replied in his stern voice, *"Who are you?"*

"I — I am my father's daughter. He is Prince Evnos of Iankoros. I don't want to be away from him. Take me to him! He'll reward you!"

The stranger's voice was softer now. "Come with me, then," he said, and took her by the hand. He led her to the only opening she had not tried. As they approached it, she saw by the lantern's light that this was not a tunnel mouth at all, but a door. The lantern bearer paused before him, put down his lantern, took a large silver key from his pocket, and opened the door.

The door creaked, and the light was like a million suns.

Amadel awoke on the floor by the table. Her father sat above her with the open book in front of him.

She caught hold of a table leg and pulled herself to her feet, then put her arms around him and wept. "Father! I'm so glad to be back. How did it happen? What was it?"

"Look." He showed her the book. The lock lay on the table, open. "You have opened it. Do you want to read now?"

"No. Not now. I was scared. I want to stay with you."

So they did not read that day, and Amadel stayed closer to her father than ever, but still she was confused. He had not rescued her, it seemed. Perhaps, she thought, he had not been able to.

Such thoughts did not occur to Prince Evnos. He congratulated himself on his little stratagem. It had been a harsh thing, but not cruel, no. To be cruel was to inflict pain without cause. This had been necessary. Now his daughter was more dependent on him than ever. That was his intention.

It did not occur to him that, in time, she might depend on someone else. Only Galthamis the Crafty could have foreseen that.

A week later they sat in the same room at the same table, and Amadel nudged the book over to her father.

"Show me."

"Now? You wish to read?"

"Yes."

"This is a great magic. Nothing is more powerful than words."

"I want to learn," she said softly, but deliberately.

"Very well, then," said Evnos. "Pick out the story you want to read."

He gave her the book and watched intently as she turned the pages in heavy handsful. He knew that there would be great significance in her choice. Much could be discerned, if one were astute enough, not merely about the meaning of the story, but about the innermost nature of the one who selected it. Therefore he smiled when he saw she had come to *The Story of the Phoenix*. He recognized the illustration even before she gave the book back to him: a picture of a golden bird chained atop a boulder, conversing with a man, while two spirits hovered in the background.

This time the meaning was easy enough to see. The Phoenix had been the emblem of the princes of Iankoros since the earliest times, and Amadel, heir to a prince, had chosen her dynasty and her realm. She had chosen well.

She looked at the picture for a long time, then asked, "What is the story about?"

"It's about the bird Phoenix," said Evnos. "You have seen its image everywhere. But now you shall know its tale. Would you like to read it?"

"Yes, but it'll take years!"

"No, it won't. You'll learn faster than that: first, the outline of the tale, then the words that make it up. So, to begin, the outline. This is the story of our first ancestor, Manahotain, the mightiest of men. He fought alongside the gods against Rannon at the beginning of time. He was there at the battle on the Plain of Leboladen, when all the gods fell before the sword of the Great Dark. Yet he held back Death that day. He fought Rannon to a draw, and the world was saved, but only at great cost. The cost is the eternal vigilance of men, who must stand alone against Rannon and the darkness. The story tells how Manahotain rescued the world, and the gods did not come to his aid. He did it alone."

"Why didn't they come?"

"Because they were dead. They had all been killed on the Plain of Leboladen. Haven't you been paying attention?"

Amadel squirmed. "Yes, but I didn't know if it was afterwards or before."

"It was afterwards, when the dust of the battle filled the sky, and the sun was the color of blood. Then Manahotain stood alone against evil. It was the year when the spring didn't come, when the snows of winter continued to pile up without melting. Snow covered the battlefield, hiding the slain, and the air was filled with snow and dust. Rivers choked with ice, and great frozen mountains wandered into the southern seas.

"All over the world, men starved. Crops could not be planted. Livestock died. Wise men conferred over the matter then, in the aftermath of Leboladen, and in the end they understood that the Phoenix had not come that year to fly over the Earth and bring the springtime, to hang in the sky and send summer's warmth, to burn itself to ashes and die in the red and orange of autumn's leaves."

"It burns up?"

"Yes, and it lies in ashes all winter long, in a kind of death, but in the earliest month of spring the ashes stir and a worm emerges. Then the worm devours the ashes and grows into the Phoenix again, and flies off into the sky to begin the summer.

"But in this year among years, the Phoenix did not come, and the Earth froze, and the great worm Shōmar circled it, breathing frigid winds onto the lands from every direction. So the wise men sent Manahotain to find the Phoenix, to bring it back, that the Earth might once more awaken.

"And Manahotain went, sore as he was, and exhausted from the battle of Leboladen. He bound up his wounds and began his journey. First, he climbed into the sky on the bridge of the rainbow, and he travelled beyond the sun, into the spaces that are always dark. There he spoke to the stars, asking them, 'Have you seen the Phoenix, the bird of summer whose plumes are like fire?' But the stars merely laughed at him, and answered, 'When one of our number expires and falls from the sky, we care not, so how could we have noticed this Phoenix?'

"Next, he returned to Earth and sailed over the seas in a boat, ever vigilant between the groaning icebergs, until he reached the southernmost land, which is barren and rightly called the Great Stone Waste. Still, weary though he was, he did not pause, but journeyed across that cold, hostile place until he came to the world's rim, and to the final precipice which drops off into nothingness. There, in the abyss, he saw the serpent Shōmar racing endlessly around the circumference of the world, chasing the golden rattles on his own tail. And Manahotain asked, 'Have you seen the Phoenix, the bird of summer with flaming plumage?' And the serpent answered, 'I see only the golden treasure before me, which I can never obtain. When I chase it quickly, it flees quickly. When I rest, it pretends to rest, only to mock me, for it is tireless. I care for nothing else. No, I have not seen the bird Phoenix. What could it matter? But if you will help me capture the gold, I will seek this Phoenix for you, out of gratitude.' Manahotain thanked him, but refused the offer, knowing that if ever Shōmar ceases to chase his tail, the Earth will no longer be bounded, and all things will slip over the edge into the void. Also, he knew that the serpent lusted after the gold and cared for nothing else, least of all gratitude.

"So, finally, Manahotain, the bravest of men, descended into the most fearsome darkness of all. Perhaps it was a deep cave. Perhaps it was the Underearth, or even a kind of dream, a darkness within his own mind; but he descended nonetheless and his courage was tested as it never had been before, even on the Plain of Leboladen. There, in the place of fear and impenetrable shadows, he discovered the Phoenix, chained to a rock with chains of ice. Spirits of Darkness and Cold stood guard over it.

"He said to them, 'Release the Phoenix. This I command you in the name of Man.'

"They replied, 'We do not fear Man. Nor shall we obey. The bird of fire is ours now.'

"And Manahotain spoke a mighty word against them, and Darkness and Cold trembled, but together *they* spoke a word of power, which counterbalanced the first. So the hero summoned another word, mightier than the first, a word which is the true name of fire and light. The Phoenix stirred at the sound of it, and for a brief instant there was a burst of light in that terrible place. Long shadows spread across the hall, and the two spirits looked like withered, bent skeletons, rippling over the rough ice and stone. Yet they replied with another word, and the absolute blackness returned.

"When he saw that he could not win this way, the hero said, 'Will you answer a riddle?'

" 'We will,' was the reply.

"So he asked them a riddle, cleverly composed, each word in it placed for the greatest power, and in that riddle were the true names of Earth and Sky, of Man, and of Life itself, and, too, all the lands of the living; and of Manahotain himself and of those minor gods which had escaped the Plain of Leboladen, those gods which still dwell upon the Earth and are known to us as clouds, as running waters, as winds, or sounds in the night.

"The sum of these Manahotain forged into one single riddle, knowing full well that all would be lost if Darkness and Cold managed to expound it. He took this great risk because he, Manahotain, the greatest of men, possessed a wit more subtle than any other.

"In the end the risk was justified. Having thus staked all, he won, for Darkness and Cold could *not* answer him. They fell aside, powerless. He drew his sword Dran — that same Dran which I now own — and cut the bonds that held the Phoenix. The bird perched for a moment upon the rock, preening its feathers, which glowed like embers. Manahotain bade it hurry away.

" 'If I return to Earth, will men honor me?' it asked.

" 'I am a man,' the hero answered.

"That was enough. The Phoenix plucked a feather out of its wing and held it out to Manahotain in its golden beak.

"He took it gingerly.

" 'Be in my favor always,' the Phoenix said. 'Find your way through all shadowed places with this, my gift.'

"Then the Phoenix flew up into the world and the snows melted and summer returned."

Prince Evnos paused, then slowly closed the book.

"That's all the story?" Amadel said.

"That is all the surface of it. Now that you know what the story is *about*, you will learn to read by studying each word and each line, until you can hear the voice of the book, and all is clear to you. Then you will know what the story *means*."

"Is there nothing more to the story?"

"As I told you. Nothing more — and everything."

"What happened next? Did he keep the feather?"

"Of course he kept it, but when he died it became — not quite real anymore, a thing of spirit. Now it manifests itself but rarely, to inspire the Princes of Iankoros or to warn them, or to remind them in times of great peril that they still enjoy the favor of the bird Phoenix."

"Have *you* ever seen it?"

"Yes," he said. He was beginning to grow exasperated. "If *course* I have."

"Oh." She sounded like she no longer quite believed him.

12 The Other

STILL MORE YEARS passed. More fruitless springtimes came. More rains and winds scoured the dead hills, until the bare stones of the island showed through.

Amadel grew from a child into a maiden, and she grew alone, with her books and such random spirits as still wandered through the castle; but her father was almost a stranger to her as he withdrew more and more into his secret researches. Sometimes after many weeks she would suddenly come upon him in a room or a corridor, or walking the battlements late at night, and he seemed more like one of the spirits, a fleeting, insubstantial thing which happened to resemble someone she once knew.

Her father had undertaken the study of the stars, and he slept by day. Once in a great while he would enter her chamber just before dawn, rouse her, and lecture passionately, obsessively about things she didn't understand at all. At those times she was afraid, and asked him no questions.

When she saw him at a distance, in dawn or in twilight, she did not call out. She did not go to him.

On cloudy nights, lights streamed from the upper windows of the Tower of Eagles. That meant he was either poring over ancient volumes, or conjuring.

Once he came to her and explained how he had discovered that the Earth itself is but a speck of dust in the great eye of Eternity.

In a blink it would be gone, unremembered. It was of no interest. Only the skies and the wandering courses of the planets were worthy of his attention.

There were fewer spirits around than before. Sometimes she only glimpsed them in the corner of her eye. She would turn suddenly and there would only be a shadow, or sunlight rippling through curtains. Sometimes she could make out a face, or the whole form of a man or a woman, but the apparition would not speak or acknowledge her in any way.

The spirits were forgetting her, and the spirits, she knew, came from her father. Therefore he was forgetting her. She was alone.

Still, she tried to do what she had been taught. The old nursemaid spirit, the first Evnos had ever conjured, had always fussed over her and told her not to let herself be unkempt. Therefore Amadel sat before her mirror every day combing her long dark hair. She dressed herself as neatly as she could, for all her gowns were often wrinkled and the starched collars drooped. They were worse after she washed her own laundry in a cistern, but there was no spirit to set things right. She could only try. She knew nothing else.

In the evenings she bathed alone in the castle bath, a huge, cold, gloomy place where spirits rustled among the eaves and sometimes sea birds fluttered beneath the ceiling.

She had no attendants now, no servants. She learned to do things for herself. She fed herself, mostly knowing that at certain hours she would usually find a meal laid out. But not always. Nothing was certain anymore. Still, she did not starve.

Her life changed even as her body changed. She accepted her increasing solitude as part of this change.

She began to take long walks over the island. She liked the open landscape, the bright, warm sun and the blue sky overhead far more than the castle's shadowed halls. She sat for long hours by the shore of the sea, staring into the distance, listening to the speech of the birds, or reading. She read, too, on her walks, sometimes stopping to scan a page intently before moving on, sometimes sitting down where she was if something particularly interested her. She spent much time atop the Black Cliffs, wondering about those places she could see across the water on a clear day, while the sea birds wheeled and cried above her. She envied the birds, wishing that she too had wings to bear her off to new lands.

She discovered the villages and towns of Iankoros and wandered through the empty houses. Sometimes she found something there, a mirror, a toy, a piece of clothing in a trunk, something that caught her fancy. She would take it back to the castle, never wondering how it came to be elsewhere. The crumbling houses were merely part of her world, like the castle itself. They had always been so.

101

Once she found a room filled with books and made several trips, dragging them behind her in a little cart.

She did not understand what any of these places had once been, anymore than she understood the overturned carriages and wagons along the roads. Some of these were filled with curious things, which she plundered and puzzled over.

But most of all, she had her books. They were her true companions, her friends. They taught her much. First she read *The Story of the Phoenix* all the way through, then all the other tales in the same volume, and she marveled at them. Each contained a whole world waiting for her. She read histories and geographies and memoirs of kings — everything she could find. She did not distinguish between true and untrue, between fact and fancy. All things were true, which the books spoke to her.

In time she came to the romances, and discovered the complex glories of *Valan and Ishurti*, the greatest love story of all. She learned from it what love was. It was a new feeling to her, almost unimaginable, a wonderful, intense longing quite unlike anything she might have once felt toward her father or the fondness she might feel for a favorite place or thing. She read of a kind of love which was feverish and incomprehensible, a little bit like madness. She read of the hero Valan's long quest over mountains and deserts, and of the weariness of the long search and the exhaustion of the soul, but also of the mystery and the joy of love and the recognition of love. She read too, and wept as she did, of the sorrow and terror of death when she shared Ishurti's last moments in the arms of the already dead Valan, in the grove of Hardath Ethor, where the wintry wind blew through the ice-laden trees and a single night owl screeched in the branches. There Ishurti wept, and died beside her lover; and for Amadel, reading as she had never read anything before, trembling, death was no longer an abstraction.

On a simpler level, the tale told her of the world beyond the ocean. She read it again and again for the descriptions, the textures, finding continual delight in the description of the grassy meadow where the hero first glimpsed his lady. Amadel had never seen a meadow. The idea of a landscape covered with living things, not conjured illusions, was more lovely than any dream or fancy.

And there were the awesome tournament scenes with their impossible, bustling crowds, thousands of spectators shouting while warriors crashed together. She knew only echoes and the cries of birds. She had never heard a multitude of voices and could not imagine even a dozen people talking at once. The roar of the scene, the sights, the sounds, the smells, all recorded in vivid detail, were a heady mixture. There were so many faces. So many people who looked different, tall, short, young and old, dressed in the garb of

102

many nationalities and social stations. She wondered how there could be so many people in all the world, let alone in one place.

Yet the book told of it, so she knew it was true.

She learned much about Iankoros from *Valan and Ishurti*, even though the island was never mentioned in the text. Her conclusions were inevitable. She read of towns, many houses clustered together along streets, and she compared them to the ruins she found in her wanderings. She saw her own world in a new way. All these roofless, windowless buildings which had been left to the wind and the rain for so many years had once comprised *towns*. People had lived there. The things she found in the houses had once belonged to someone other than herself, other than her father.

All had changed somehow. The people had gone away. The *meadows* had gone away, leaving bare earth and stone behind.

Yet her father said nothing about any of this. Once she dared interrupt him during one of his twilight walks. She asked, because she could no longer bear not knowing. But he was angry when she did, and that frightened her.

"Nothing ever changes," he shouted, waving his hands. "Go away. Don't think about it. Don't bother me. Iankoros is as it always was and always will be."

With each rereading of *Valan and Ishurti*, the mystery deepened.

Again she read of the Great Stone Waste, and, in the book of tales, of King Thillamdel's hopeless search for the land of youth, which is called Elimdorath the Beautiful. From such accounts she learned that ships were wooden houses that moved across water, borne by their sails the way wings bear a bird. She understood that the *ships* she saw in the distance had *people* in them.

It occurred to her that the folk of Iankoros might have gone away in ships, but she could not explain why they had left, or why they never ventured near their homes again.

Once more she saw things in a new light: the harbor, the rotting quays, the bare masts sticking out of the water. She recognized the ruins of ships even as she had the ruins of houses, and understood that no one had sailed away.

She got another idea from a minor, fragmentary narrative, *The Bird-Summoned One*, in which the heroine is imprisoned atop a mountain, and, knowing the secret language of the birds, is able to tell them her plight and send for the hero.

Amadel began to look longingly at the gulls as they circled overhead or swooped over the ocean to snatch up fish. She wasn't like the heroine. She didn't think she needed to be rescued, but she could use the same device to communicate with other lands. So she went to her father and asked to be taught the speech of the birds.

She discovered him in his study. Although it was still afternoon, the place was lighted with tapers. All the windows were shuttered and bolted.

In the half-light Prince Evnos seemed very old. He was pale and thin and his hair and beard were going gray. Amadel had only a vague idea how people aged, but it didn't seem right to her. Her father was like one of those deserted shells of houses she had found, empty, worn down by the weather.

"Father," she said softly. "You are the greatest magician in the world. Surely you can teach me to speak to things that aren't people — like animals, and birds."

He snorted. It wasn't a laugh, just a snort.

"I *am* the greatest magician in the world. There is no doubt about that. At times I have thought that you too, my daughter, would be a great magician. At other times I decided not. I thought you could not bear to even hear about the things I have done. It would drive you mad with the terror of it. Yet from those deeds I have gained great wisdom. Isn't that odd? I have learned that nothing matters, not love, not magic, not deeds, not even wisdom. This knowledge has arisen before me, like a flower out of a dung heap. No, not even that. What does the universe care about flowers and dung heaps and men? All are swirling motes in an uneasy wind. They'll be gone soon. Has their brief moment together any significance?"

He did not seem to expect an answer. His voice trailed off and he sat at his desk, staring into the shadows somewhere behind her.

She stuck to her original intent.

"Father, can you do it? Can you talk to the birds?"

Another snort. "Why should I bother? That's the simplest form of magic. Any village witch can do that. It you want a cow cured of its disease, call a witch. If you want to jabber with sparrows, call a witch."

"But there aren't any witches here, even if there are villages. Or were."

He was suddenly alert. "What do you mean by that?"

"Those empty houses all together. They must have been villages once."

"Well, pay them no mind, girl. Everything you'll ever need or want is here, in this castle. The houses have always been empty. Always will be. Nothing changes. Ever."

"Can you . . . teach me?"

He sighed. "Yes, I can teach you. I think it might even be a good idea."

Suddenly he was up from his desk and pacing about the room, more alive than she had seen him in a long time. "Yes, yes, it's a fine idea. I had hoped for this. I had planned to teach you magic.

104

Yes. But how could I know if you had any *talent* for magic unless we *begin*, and we can't begin unless you express a *will* to learn. I can't force it on you. It has to be your own choosing. That's the beginning of all magic."

So he taught her. Their sessions were long and intense. He would not let her leave, even when she was tired or distracted. They slept in that upper room, in the Tower of Eagles. Spirits brought them food, and once, when she complained, a tub of steaming bathwater for Amadel.

Evnos drove her on, as if, it seemed to her, he too were desperately struggling for something. His lectures were like those sudden, impassioned monologues of years before.

He went on for five days like that. It seemed to her that her father had somehow *come awake* during that brief period.

Then it was over, and he went back to sleep again, if that was the right analogy. His mind descended into a torpor. He said to her very softly, "Now you are finished with this. It is a trivial thing. It won't do you any good. But it is only a beginning."

Then he opened a book and returned to his studies as if she were no longer in the room.

She left, uncertain and a little frightened. She was eager to try out her new knowledge, but was not sure what she wanted to do with it. Her purpose had been clear enough before. Now she was confused.

It was mid-afternoon. She walked toward the Black Cliffs and arrived there at sunset. The sky was already darkening to the east, the mainland a barely discernible blue-black line on the horizon. To the west, the sea and sky flared into reds and oranges and purples.

She called out to the birds of the air, summoning them to herself out of the sky and from the cliffs, hailing them with a cry used by one of their number to locate the flock in darkness or in fog.

The birds came. They swarmed around her, wings whirring, not at all afraid of this strange human who spoke their language.

She offered them fish scraps. They covered the ground at her feet, a jostling, white blanket spread out for yards. The air was thick with feathers.

After they had eaten, she questioned them.

"Speak to me, wind-borne friends, of the lands beyond the sea."

"They are far, far, away," the birds answered, clucking and squawking, somehow forming a single voice. "The flight is tiring. How your wings ache! Unless you can find a rising current. Then you can glide all the way."

"But what is in those lands, soaring brothers? Tell me of the people, the cities, the great ships and castles."

105

Wings fluttered. Less harmonious now, in a babble of individual voices, the birds replied, "Wide, wide land. Goes on forever. Don't like to go that far from the water. There's a river. You can follow the river."

"The ships! The ships! If you're very tired and the wind won't carry you, sometimes you can find a ship and rest on its wind-trees, and the ship will take you where you're going. That's what ships are for."

"Sometimes sailors chase you away."

"Or try to eat you!"

"A curse on men that eat us!"

"Please, please," said Amadel. "I don't care about those things. I want to know — I want to know all about the people in those lands, what they do, how they live."

"What they do? What they do?" said the birds.

"There is a big dock in the city," the birds continued, "by the river, by the running brown water, by the soft, gentle-speaking river. You can float there. You can wait every morning for the man with the wobbly round body, the man like a bird with no wings, who comes to throw fish parts into the water. The best parts. *Then* the eating is good!"

"Sometimes he doesn't come. Sometimes a little man does."

"A boy."

"And all through the city are places where the eating is also good. Humans throw away such delicious entrails!"

"Guts!"

Amadel waved her hands furiously. "I don't want to hear about fish guts!" she shouted. "I want to hear about kings and heroes and adventures."

"Who cares about those? You can't eat them."

Amadel saw that it was hopeless. She thanked the birds and dismissed them. She turned back toward the castle. It was a long walk. She knew she was too tired to make it.

Halfway across the island, she found one of the villages. There was an inn at the end of the main street which still had a roof, of wood and tiles rather than thatch. She slept there, on a soft, slightly moldering bed.

A dream came to her. She knew that she was dreaming, but that did not make the experience any less intense, or the dream any less true.

A voice called her name.

"Amadel. Amadel. Come here."

"Here I am," she said, sitting up in the dream. "I am coming."

For a moment she seemed bound to the bed, but with a great heave

106

she got up. Something tore, then gave way. She stood by the side of the bed and looked down at herself, her body, still asleep.

Her dreaming self left the room, going where the voice bade her, down a flight of stairs, across the common room, and outside. The Black Cliffs loomed over her. She was on the beach. Cold wind from the ocean touched her as if she were naked. The sound of the surf was like a giant's breathing.

The moon rose, brilliant and white and full, and by its light she saw a great ship far out at sea, as huge as a castle, its white-gold sails flapping like the wings of a bird. It drew ever nearer until its vastness seemed to fill the very sky, blotting out the stars and the moon.

Then, somehow, she was on the deck of that ship. Overhead, sails and rigging groaned, but the deck underfoot was as solid and motionless as the Black Cliffs.

Huge birds swarmed around her, walking on human legs, their folded wings glowing in the moonlight like soft white gowns. She wandered among them as they paced back and forth, trying to speak to them, but they ignored her, babbling, clucking, turning their heads away sharply as she approached.

"Amadel, come here," the voice called again.

She followed the sound and came to a hatchway, then descended a ladder, groping uncertainly for the rungs in the dark. At the bottom was a damp place that stank of fish. In the gloom she could barely make out a single, large wooden crate in the middle of the floor.

Here, unlike on the deck above, the floor beneath her swayed from side to side. The crate scraped slowly in one direction, then another.

"Amadel."

The voice was coming out of the crate. She went over to it. The lid rose of its own accord.

Her father lay inside, half buried in sand and gravel, his face pale, sunken, his hands crossed on his breast. As her eyes adjusted and she could make out more, she saw that he was surrounded with rich treasure, heaps of gold coins and jewels, fine garments, and his sword, Dran, in its scabbard by his side.

His eyes were open. He stared at the ceiling. He did not turn to look at her as she approached. He merely seemed to know she was there.

"Everything you shall ever want, my Amadel, is here, on this island of Iankoros. You are a princess of this land. Remember that. Remember too that you are your father's daughter. Remember that most especially."

"Yes," she said. "I will remember it."

Then she was no longer in the ship. For an instant, she stood on the beach, watching as the huge vessel faded into transparency like rising mist. The night wind was cold. The frigid water lapped around her ankles.

She turned to go, and found herself at the inn. There had been no transition, not a single step taken. She was merely there, at the base of the stairs in the common room. She climbed to her chamber, then stood over her sleeping self. Gradually, somehow, she came to be lying in the bed again, half-awake in the first light of dawn.

Still she gazed at the ships almost daily. She desperately wanted one of them to come near the island, to reveal its mysteries to her, but they only skirted the horizon for a little while before vanishing.

She waited for something to happen, not even truly discontented, but merely uneasily curious. She wanted to see what was beyond the horizon for all that, in a sense, she was afraid to see.

At last a ship came to her.

One midsummer night all the world shook with a storm's fury, and from where she watched from her high window, Amadel saw the stark landscape revealed for an instant in a flash of lightning, then sheathed again in darkness. The rain pounded, almost roared on the roofs. Here and there little streams poured through, splashing on the floor.

The spray from the open window drenched her, but still she watched, expectant, somehow aware that this particular tempest was not like all the others. Her father had told her once that the first and greatest talent of the magician was the ability to sense the true meanings of events. That much she had inherited from him. She sensed a meaning strongly now, an alienness, an intrusion.

The rain rippled like dark curtains before the window. Far away, the white-capped waves crashed against the island, one after another, whole legions of them, thundering against rocks hidden from her sight by nearby cliffs. And on this night the wind blew through that narrow channel that led into the harbor, like breath blowing across the mouth of a bottle. It seemed that the island itself cried out.

She sat all night by the window, never once glimpsing her father or any of his wraiths. In time she did not hear the thunder, and the flashes and the darkness were as one. She fell asleep in the early morning hours and awoke at midday, her head on the windowsill, her hair heavy with rainwater.

The storm had abated. The sky was gray above her, the darkest clouds, ragged with streamers, scattering beneath the higher and paler overcast.

She rose stiffly, drying her face and hair with a towel. She went into the kitchen, where a meal had been laid out. She ate in silence, alone, warming herself with hot tea, holding the cup between her hands as she sat staring at the tabletop.

Then she hurried out into the muddy world, pulled up her skirt, and waded barefoot across the drenched land, often sinking to her knees, until she came to a path that led down to a rocky beach.

She had always looked forward to storms. They were special treats, occasions for finding strange objects washed up on the shore afterwards, novelties from the lands beyond the sea.

This time something truly extraordinary was deposited for her examination: a great vessel had been cast upon a reef a little way out from the narrow beach. The rocks had ripped the ship's bottom out, and it lay on its side, awash in the receding tide, its hull like a partially crushed egg. Both masts had snapped away, and wreckage was strewn all along the water's edge.

Amadel hurried down to the shoreline, delirious with excitement. It was as if the entire, hidden world had been thrown upon her island all at once. Barrels and crates bobbed in the shallows, containing she knew not what. Each one she would open in time.

First she came to some spars, a tangle of rigging, shattered planking, a broken cask filled with seawater, and then a man lying face down in the shallows, the water lapping around his shoulders. She paused uneasily at the sight of the corpse, not quite afraid, but unhappy now. The rush of excitement was gone. She did not entirely understand what the corpse was. Aside from her father, this was the only human being she had ever seen. It was all confusing, an abstraction.

She came upon more debris, whole sections of deck or hull cast at odd angles on the shore. There were more drowned sailors, some of them with crushed heads and limbs bent, as if they were rag dolls destroyed by an angry child.

Pale, blank faces stared up at Amadel through the shallow water.

She stepped around the corpses carefully, still searching for strange treasures from distant lands. A large trunk floated a little way out from the beach. She waded in to grab it, lost hold of her skirt, fell, and got thoroughly wet, banging an elbow painfully on a stone in the process. On all fours for an instant, coughing from seawater she had swallowed, she reached out for the trunk's handle, caught it, and pulled herself to her feet. She began to drag the trunk toward the beach.

Just as she got it onto the sand, she heard someone cough. She stopped, frozen.

"Who's there?"

Another cough. One of the limp figures moved slightly. "Help me," said a feeble voice. She lost all interest in the trunk and ran to where the stranger lay on his back in the water, gasping and sputtering as the surf washed over him. It was a boy, entangled in rigging and clinging to a piece of mast. He was about her own age or a little younger, thin, deathly pale, with a look of infinite exhaustion on his face.

Amadel's heart beat wildly. She stood, staring down at him, unsure of what to do in this completely unprecedented situation. She was actually, for the first time in her life, in the presence of someone from beyond Iankoros. If he should die — No! He would not die!

She fumbled excitedly with the ropes until she got him free, dragged him by the arms onto the beach. There she let him drop onto his back and could only watch as he lay still for a minute, then rolled over, vomiting seawater. For several minutes he remained as he was, breathing hard, oblivious to her.

She was still at a loss. She could not find any words. At last she managed, "Are you — all right?"

He turned onto his back and looked up at her, too tired to be surprised. "Yes. I think so."

"Can I — do anything?"

"Do you have any water?"

His voice was hoarse.

For an instant she was puzzled, and was about to point out the whole ocean full of water — but then she understood.

"Yes. There's a spring in a cave near here. Should I fetch some water for you?"

The boy lurched to his feet and Amadel caught him as he nearly fell. He staggered, leaning on her, and looked up wearily at the naked cliffs, the barren hills, and the gray sky.

"What a dreary place. What country is this? Last night in the storm we didn't know where we were. We saw the cliffs and the captain said it might be Iankoros and everybody was so afraid —"

"But this *is* Iankoros," said Amadel, her voice trailing away in doubt. It was incomprehensible to her that anyone should be afraid of the place she knew only as home.

The boy let out a cry of horror and pulled away from her. He ran a short distance, then stopped, barely able to stand. She wondered if he might be insane. She had read about mad people in books, and knew that such people did strange things for no reason. She hurried over to him.

"Where are you going?"

"Nowhere," he said with resignation. He glanced toward the many corpses bobbing in the surf. "I'm dead like them, only worse. The ones who drowned are better off."

Now Amadel was almost certain that he was, indeed, mad, and she was, more than anything else, angry at the storm for bringing her a mad boy, of all possible visitors from the outside world.

110

She spoke very cautiously. "What are you talking about? Isn't it better to be alive?"

"But this is *Iankoros*, isn't it? Doesn't Prince Evnos live here?"

"He does. I am his daughter."

"What? How —? The evil wizard of Iankoros has a *daughter?*"

She took him by the arm again. He flinched, but did not resist. "He isn't evil," she said gently. "He is the greatest magician in the world."

Now he did pull away again, and the fear in his voice was very real.

"Then stay away from me — she-monster! What are you *really?* Didn't your father sell all his people to the Dark One so he could live forever? Doesn't he serve Rannon even now, by sending out curses and plagues into the world?"

She was quite certain now. Yes, he was mad. She didn't know whether to be angry *with him* or to regard him as one afflicted, like a gull with a broken wing.

"No," she said. "He doesn't do any of those things."

"But everybody knows it! When little children are bad, their mothers tell them *Now you be good or wicked Prince Evnos will steal you and give you to Rannon!* People know it everywhere in the world."

"Those are lies!" said Amadel, bewildered, hurt. Here was a stranger, someone she had been looking forward to meeting all her life, and, mad or not, he had no business telling horrible lies about her father.

The boy's voice dropped to a whisper. He wasn't arguing. He was terribly afraid. He trembled. Amadel thought he was going to fall over, and reached out again to catch him. But he drew back, albeit slowly this time.

"Didn't he . . . ? Didn't he send you down here to catch anyone who might be left, so he could torture them?"

"No. He doesn't know I'm here. Or that you are. I don't see him much anymore. He's always in his tower with his books."

This seemed to reassure the newcomer. After a few minutes more, he let Amadel touch him, and said nothing as she led him into the cave, halfway up the cliff face and reached by a narrow path. Within, spring water poured down the rocks, into a pool. The boy knelt beside the pool and drank deeply.

Then he sat back and looked at Amadel cautiously.

"Are you really his daughter?"

"Yes. Didn't I tell you I was?"

She did not understand this questioning. Then she reminded herself that he was mad. But she did not really believe that, and was more aware than ever that she knew almost nothing about the people of the rest of the world.

111

"I — I never knew he had a daughter. None of the stories say he does."

"Well, he does."

"Who was your mother?"

That question hit Amadel like an unexpected blow. She couldn't answer. She sat, fidgeting, staring up at the cave ceiling. This was a subject she had somehow, always, shut out from her mind.

At last she said, "I don't know. Father wouldn't tell me much about her, and he always became angry when I asked. So I stopped asking. I know her name was Riacinera, and I look like her."

"They say — the people back home — that he had a wife named Riacinera, but he gave her to Rannon as a sacrifice, to save his own life during a plague. They say he's terribly evil. A monster. They say he drinks blood."

"He's not. He's just very . . . distant. He shuts himself away a lot, but he isn't evil. I can remember times when he was loving. When I was little."

"Have you always lived here alone?"

"Not alone. With him."

The boy pondered this.

"Maybe some of the stories are wrong. Part of them anyway. You said he doesn't know I'm here. Please, just for now at least, don't tell him. You rescued me and I owe you a lot, and I guess I shouldn't ask anything from you, but I have to. Keep me a secret, for a little while."

"If you want," said Amadel.

"Can I stay here, in this cave? Can you bring me food every day?"

"I can get you food right now. Are you hungry?"

"Yes."

He seemed wary of her again. She was aware of him watching her closely as she walked to he mouth of the cave, stopped, and called out a series of words. Then she came back in, sat down beside him, and said, "Now, just wait."

And after a pause she said, "Don't be afraid."

He forced a smile.

A tiny cloud of smoke drifted into the cave, gathered into a sphere, expanded, then burst like a bubble. A man stood there, dressed in the uniform of the palace servants. He held a basket. At a sign from Amadel, he set down the basket, then vanished as suddenly as he had appeared.

The boy looked at her with wonder. "So you're a magician too!"

"You only have to know the right words. Father taught me."

She wanted to ask him why there were no such spirits where he came from, and she did not want to reveal how ignorant she was of the ways of the world.

112

"Does your father — conjure them?" the boy asked.

"When he needs them."

"Then won't the — ghost tell him I'm here?"

"Oh no. They're too stupid to remember anything."

He removed the covering from the basket. Within were bread, eggs, smoked meat, and a flask of wine.

"Is it real food?"

"Try it."

He took a bite of the bread, then stared at her with wide eyes. She watched him eat as if she had never seen anyone eat before. He was so nervous he could hardly swallow.

The boy's name was Menas; and Amadel kept him in the cave, her own private secret. He could not remember the name of his father, he told her, and his mother had died of plague when he was small. When he was six he was sold to a sea captain, who first made him a serving boy, then an apprentice, and finally gave him his freedom and made him his son. Amadel did not ask how it was possible to be the son of two, even three people at once. But she questioned him on other things, and was relieved to find that his answers were much, much more interesting than those of the gulls.

He had sailed all over the world with the captain, he said, visiting strange places filled with wonders. He had continued sailing, barely spending any time on land, until the night of the storm. There had been a desperate struggle to guide the ship away from the black cliffs of the unknown coast, whither the wind and current seemed determined to drive it. Hours of wet toil ended suddenly with the heavy grinding that all sailors fear, the trembling of the whole ship when the keel has struck something solid. Then came the rending of decks, headlong tumbling, an endless battle to stay above the raging sea, voices crying far off, and unconsciousness. When it was over, he awoke to find waves lapping around his ears and a web of ropes over his face.

He told Amadel all he could of the world and its many peoples, all the good things and much of the evil mixed in together. It hardly bothered her that the things he described were not much like those of the glittering romances. His words were, to her, like a new and wholly different kind of book, and she accepted this new tale as she would any other. There were so many mysteries in what he said. Perhaps, in time, she would understand them. For now, she just listened.

Sometimes he would describe something exactly as she expected, and then his account had a special kind of excitement. He had indeed been to a tournament in the city of Nedek, very much like the one in *Valan and Ishurti*. There really *were* thick forests and green

113

meadows on the mainland. This was more fantastic than even the idea of the tournament. She knew seaweed, of course, but had never seen grass, much less a tree. All the things she had dreamt about, the forests and rivers and snow-capped mountains, the huge cities crowded with people, all became completely solid, utterly real, now that he told her of them.

In turn she spoke about her own life, of her flight into the sky, of the island and its many spirits. He could not conceal his amazement, and seemed to be a little afraid of her again. But this passed. She hoped she did not fit his idea of what an evil, magical person was like. She hoped her father didn't either. She wanted to introduce him to her father one day.

Meanwhile, she brought him some books, and was astonished to learn that he could not read. His education had been the world, not from the written page. So she read to him and tried to teach him letters.

Every day she visited him in the cave, always bringing something from the castle, food or clothing or books, or sometimes some artifact she thought he would find interesting. They spent long hours together sitting in the cave mouth above the narrow beach. They watched the waves pick away at the broken hulk of the ship until there was nothing left of it. Sometimes, at night, they walked along the beach, or inland, along the barren roads, among the empty houses. But he was always unhappy about these trips, refusing to come within sight of the castle, afraid that somehow her father would see him. Amadel did not force him to continue.

They became friends, and slowly, inevitably, as their lives were filled with one another, they learned to love. A touch lingered longer, then became a touch of a different sort, and ultimately led to something in which both of them were altogether ignorant. In the end, they coupled there on the rough, pebble-strewn floor of the cave, and this was the greatest of many wonders.

Amadel still saw her father sometimes at meals. He left her entirely unsupervised, but occasionally she would come into the dining hall expecting to find a meal laid out, or prepared to command the spirits to make one for her to take back to share with Menas, and instead find Evnos waiting for her, already seated.

Somehow, he knew when she was coming. He still maintained the rituals of the court of Iankoros. When custom demanded it, on the feast days of the lesser gods, or on the days set aside in honor of the heroes, he would dine with her in the great hall, while many shapes would rush about serving. Sometimes ghostly guests sat at the other tables. The hall would fill with barely perceptible lords and ladies in splendid costumes, and Amadel and Evnos would sit among them, dressed in their own finery, while conjured musicians played faint tunes on instruments made of candleflame and shadow.

A short while after Menas's arrival, Amadel encountered her father in the hall, at dusk. She was startled, since this was no special day, but she was too hungry and tired to make anything of it. She had spent the whole day with her friend, exploring the intricacies of the island's caves, and astounding him with the few tricks of illusion she knew.

Her father sat on his high throne at the head of the table. Tapestries billowed from the walls in a sudden draught. Her footsteps echoed.

The Prince indicated that she should sit beside him, and she sat. They ate in silence for a while. She dared not tell him what she had been doing, but she wanted to hear his voice, to know if she could still understand his words. Suddenly she was terribly anxious. But he would not speak to her.

Then she asked him a question, and another, but he stared into the distance as if she were not there.

She glanced to the other end of the hall. Dust stirred. A tapestry shifted.

She fell silent once more. She did not understand her father. As the years went by, she knew, he became stranger and more distant. But this, in itself, did not frighten her. She told herself it was for the best. He was a learned man, the greatest wizard in the world. He was perhaps considering some profound question of philosophy or magic, and could not be distracted by her chattering. Yes, that was it. Some abstruse matter. She could not interrupt.

And yet she felt a very real fear, and had to force herself to eat and remain by his side.

It was only at the end of the meal, as the Prince rose to depart, that he said anything. He stared intently at the still seated Amadel and spoke in a voice that lacked all human expression, like a wind between stones.

"Let not the fine metal be tempered with the base. It gains no strength that way."

He left the room without another word. She knew better than to follow him and ask what he meant. He had said all he intended to. She was more afraid than ever.

She did not mention any of this to Menas the following morning, when she brought him food, but her father's words never left her mind, like some all-important riddle she had to solve, but could not.

She spent the day with her friend at the cave's mouth, poring over a book. She was still fascinated by what Menas could tell her about the world, but at the same time, from their readings, from the questions he asked, she was aware that she knew many things he did not.

It was only fair, then, that they trade information. Today she was teaching him to read, as she herself had been taught. She told him part of the story of the epic of Iankoros, *The Song of the Great Stone*, and it excited him greatly. Then she showed him the opening of the poem in a book, and taught him to understand it word by word, line by line, until it was clear to him and they could move on to another section.

It was a bright day with a gentle breeze, and they sat undisturbed throughout the length of it, reading from the book, their feet dangling over the ledge above the beach.

One of the brainless spirits brought lunch.

That night Evnos was once more seated at the dinner table, and again he spoke only once, at the very end. This time there was there was a trace of sternness in his voice.

He said, "The Princess of Iankoros is a sacred person."

She was troubled. The drift of his meaning was becoming clear.

On the third evening his tone was one of barely suppressed anger. That was when he said, "The power of the virgin is very great."

13 A Prisoner

THAT NIGHT Amadel watched her father's window from her own. Lights burned in his study until very late. They were still there when she dozed off. This encouraged her. It meant that he was locked away with his secret labors and he would be up till dawn, then sleep through the day. She would not be seen leaving the castle in the morning.

A few hours later she rose, breakfasted quickly, and ran to the cave where Menas waited. She roused him and said breathlessly, "You'll have to leave. My father knows you're here. And he's angry."

The boy sat up, obviously terrified. Amadel had told him again and again that her father was a kind, not a wicked man, but clearly Menas had never believed her. Indeed, her own distress seemed to confirm his worst fears.

"But how? How do I get away?"

"Build a boat or something," said Amadel.

"With what?"

She paused. She had never actually considered how boats were built.

"Could you do something with the wood from the one that was wrecked? There's still a lot lying around."

"Yes. I suppose so. A raft at least. I'll have to. Maybe I can get out to where a ship could pick me up. I mean, where it could pick *us* up."

"Us?"

"Don't you want to get away from this horrible place?"

"Yes, but —"

"But what? Hurry. We don't have much time."

Again she hesitated, puzzled, afraid. She had thought of leaving the island many times, but those thoughts had always been abstractions, not something she would actually set out immediately and *do*. Now, the actual possibility in front of her was more frightening than she could ever have imagined.

"I'm . . . I'm princess here," she said. "That's very important."

"You're princess of *what?*"

"Of Iankoros. The Princess of Iankoros is a sacred person."

"But, can't you see? There *isn't* any Iankoros anymore. It's dead. No one lives here. It's just mud and rocks and ruins. If you stay, you'll live your life alone, and you'll grow old alone. You'll be bent and ugly and you'll never have known what it's like to be *really alive* at all. You won't have any children, any family, anything except an empty castle that's slowly falling down. You'll be old there alone. You'll get sick alone, and eventually you'll die, alone. You told me once that you wanted to get away from here more than anything else. Why can't you, now that there's a chance?"

She paced back and forth, playing nervously with her hair.

"I — I don't know what to do." She began to weep. "I don't want to be alone, but I —"

He stood up and took her hand in his, then drew her close.

"Look," he said. "You know what's happened. It's something that happens to the noble knights and ladies in the books, at the end of their adventures. But it's not just for them. It's happened to *us* now, right here. I love you, Amadel, and I don't want to go away without you. Where would I go? I have no one. The captain and the sailors are drowned. Please . . ."

"All right. I'll go, because —"

"Because?"

"Because I love you too," she said quietly.

They rose to leave. At that instant thunder crashed just outside the cave and both of them were blinded by a burst of searing light. Wind roared past their ears. Then came the sound of huge wings. When Amadel could see again, she looked in horror at the figures now filling the cave mouth.

It was her father, terrible in his wrath, and behind him crouched a monstrous ape-thing with arms thicker than a man's body, and flabby wings folded onto its back. The creature opened its mouth and snarled, fangs an explosion of white in a black face.

Amadel shrieked. Menas stood frozen.

First Prince Evnos addressed the boy. "Do you like my monkey?

He'll take you away from here. Don't worry. You won't have to stay long." Then to his daughter he said, "He *knows?* The legendary, wicked sorcerer Evnos *knows?* Yes, yes, he has known. Has he not eyes and ears in his own land, in the kingdom you have defiled? Did he not know *from the first* that his daughter was a traitor and a harlot? Did he not watch her in his perspective glass when she polluted herself and her name and her lineage? And did he not wait until exactly the correct moment to deliver exactly the correct punishment? He did. Indeed, he did!"

She felt sick. She wanted to die. It was torture to speak even a word. But she could only think of Menas.

"Father, what will you do to him?"

"To him? You ask about him before yourself? What does it matter what I do to him? He is common refuse, washed up by the sea. The world is filled with such already. But once you were different. Now—"

"Father, don't hurt him!"

"Get out of this cave! Go!" Before she could reply the thunder came again, and the floor heaved beneath her feet. She was falling, stones rattling around her. Again, a blinding light —

Suddenly she was outside, halfway down the path to the beach with no memory of having walked there. She stumbled and fell on rough stones, then turned and looked up. The ape crouched between her and the cave mouth. It turned toward her and snarled.

Then the creature went into the cave, and she heard her father shriek, "You'd have my daughter? No! No! But you can have my ape!"

Menas screamed, long and horribly. The sound was unlike anything Amadel had ever heard before.

A moment later the ape emerged with the limp boy in its arms.

Evnos followed. "Take him!" he said. "Take him where you will!" The beast spread its wings and rose heavily into the air. Then its wingbeat increased to a thundering blur and the creature darted off, as quickly and suddenly as an enormous bee.

Amadel hadn't been able to see Menas clearly. There had been only a fleeting impression: his pale face, one arm hanging at a strange angle, blood all down his front.

In only seconds the ape had diminished to a black dot in the sky, far out over the sea.

She wept uncontrollably, falling to her knees, striking the ground with her fists, tearing her hair. Dimly she was aware that her father had come down the path, that he stood over her.

"Defiled one," he said softly, terribly, "whose name I shall never more utter, from this day forward you shall never leave my castle.

I shall set a charm against you on all the doors, gates, and windows, and while I live you shall not go out."

He took her by the arm and set off for the castle at an unrelenting pace. They walked half the day, it seemed. She begged him to stop, to let her rest, to just leave her alone to return when she would; but he strode on, unspeaking, as if fully ready to tear her arm from her shoulder and not even pause.

Her father had spoken the truth. From that day forward, none of the gates to the outside would open for her. She tried them all, hoping that in his madness, in his distraction, he had forgotten one; but he had been very thorough.

Once, she spied a rectangle of light at the end of a secret passageway and ran toward it. She knew this door. It had never been closed in all her lifetime. The hinges were rusted solid. For an instant, then, hope returned, and she ran with all her might, in desperate silence.

But when she drew near, the rust fell from the hinges and the door swung at her with a low moan, slamming hard into her face as though of its own volition.

She fell to the floor with a bloodied nose and wept. It seemed that all she did was weep anymore.

She wandered throughout the castle, her hair uncombed, her clothing torn and dirty. She looked ceaselessly for a way out, like an cat pacing back and forth in a cage, for all she knew it was hopeless.

Once she sat in a courtyard near the outer wall, and on a sudden impulse heaved up one of the flagstones, then dug in the dirt underneath with her hands, furiously, until her nails were broken and bleeding and her arms were smeared with mud. Weeping again, she lay by the hole in the evening and slept. She awoke once in the middle of the night, saw the light in her father's window as usual, then laughed, then cried, then sang nonsense to herself. She told herself that all was as it had once been, that nothing would ever change. She thought she was going mad and welcomed it. She prayed to what little gods there might be who could cloud her dreams, hoping to find relief in madness, but even this was denied her.

Still, she found time to read her books. Only one of them was true to her anymore, Onda Rithon's *The Tale of the Black Mountain*. She read it again and again. The evil wizard in the story was very real — he was Prince Evnos — and his hopeless captive was herself. The ending seemed her own inevitable doom. She lingered over the final scene, where the despairing maiden drowned herself beneath a waterfall and her hair and gown spread out in the water like the petals of some beautiful, broken flower.

Amadel had no mountain pool, no waterfall, and the moat of the

Phoenix Nest was long empty. She could not even reach the sea, but she was still resolved to end her life. She was clear-headed about this. Her hysteria was past. It was no longer time for weeping. Carefully she considered which towers she could jump from, how many high windows there were, how many ledges. A crash to the stone pavement below would suffice. She thought of herself as a statue tumbling end over end in the air, breaking to bits as it struck.

She waited until a night when there was no moon, when the stars alone would witness her deed. She remembered Menas. She had thought of little else for days, savoring again and again every word, every texture of each instant she shared with him. She didn't know what happened to people after death. The books were vague. Her father wouldn't tell her. Even back when he had told her many things, he had always evaded this point. But in some of the romances, lovers were reunited after they died. She hoped for that. There could be no other hope. She did not have to consciously admit what she already knew — that Menas was dead.

She went to the window of her own room and sat on the sill, letting her legs dangle into the space beyond. She looked up at the stars she would never see again, at the towers and roofs of the castle that had once been the whole world to her, and began to repeat the words of a melancholy song, chanting them with hardly any tune.

"The white bird flies so high.
The black bird flies higher —
Oh, never, never, never!
I shall not fly with them.
They will not wait for me.
Oh, never, never, never!
Oh never, never, never!
I have no wings to fly with,
And my heart cannot be free."

It was time. She took a deep breath, as if to dive into water, and pushed herself off.

The sensation of falling was like flight in a dream, gentle, drifting, beautiful. The windows whirled around her, and above her the stars were spinning streaks. Her hair and clothing streamed from her, spinning, spinning. She saw the pavement rushing up to meet her.

"Stop!" It was her father's voice. The very air shook with it. She thought she saw his face glaring down at her from behind the stars, huge as the sky.

Then the air was frigid as icewater, and for an instant she hung dangling awkwardly, a foot or so above the pavement. Mist closed around her, and she began to rise, slowly at first, then faster, as

121

spirits formed in the mist, their forms shifting like smoke, but their hands solid enough as they bore her past endless stones, past windows, into her own room. One of them was her old nursemaid, the one created from mud and dust. She hadn't seen that face in years.

"My foolish, foolish, little girl," the maid said over and over. Her voice had always been soothing before. Now it was scolding.

She came to rest gently on her own bed. Still she was cold, in a delirium. The spirits whispered around her. Then the mist dispersed, and she was alone in darkness.

After a while she sat up and beheld a faint wisp lingering over the windowsill. She didn't doubt it would thicken if she tried to jump again, that the vapor would become iron bars. She lay back on the bed.

So she couldn't even die. Did he truly control everything? He would watch her closely now. She would never get another chance to hurl herself from a height. Or to do anything else, she was certain. Some spirit would knock poison from her hand or snatch away a dagger.

The next few days were like a dream. She felt nothing. She only saw things in a detached way, as if from a great distance. She was not a part of the world around her. The spirits now congregated in her rooms, but it was as if *she* were the phantom and they the living people.

She tried to tell herself that she was beyond all hurting, that she had shed her pain like a veil, that nothing mattered anymore. Again, she became, in a way, clear-headed. She merely observed, making no attempt to understand what was going on around her. She watched, completely alone, for all the spirits were with her always, even though her father lingered somewhere in the castle. She was alone.

On a clear morning, half an hour after dawn, she watched her father cross the yard below her window. He moved slowly, like a sleepwalker. Mist still clung to the ground. She leaned out the window to see better, and vapors gathered around her, thicker and thicker.

She thought for a moment that he was coming toward her, up to her room, but he did not come. After a few minutes, she leaned back in, and sat still, wondering what he might be doing. The mystery of it was enough to make her want to follow him. She wasn't eager or afraid, or filled with any emotion at all. But the novelty stirred her. She too moved like a sleepwalker.

By the time she reached the yard below, he was far away, vanishing down a passage, around a corner. She ran to catch up, silent in her bare feet. The morning air was frigid through her thin, tattered gown. The pavement felt like a rough sheet of ice. She hugged herself for warmth.

Evnos had reached the armory and gone inside. She trailed after, more slowly now, into almost total darkness. The place had been shuttered for a long time, and the floor beneath her feet was gritty with dust and burningly cold.

Her eyes adjusted slowly, and she made out her father at the far end of the room, pressing on a certain stone in the wall. Then he was gone, and a doorway gaped where the wall had been. She lingered in the shadows for a while, until she was sure he had travelled a good distance along the new passage, then followed.

The gently sloping floor inside was so cold it burned. Still she groped her way along, stretching out her arms to touch either side of the tunnel as she went. There was no light at all until, far ahead, a witchlight sparked at the tip of her father's finger. He held it up to light a candle.

Still she followed, breathing hard, but in utter silence as the passage wound slowly down into the heart of the island. At times she thought she could hear the sea. At times there was no sound at all except her father's shuffling step and the beating of her own heart. At last they came to a door which opened at the Prince's approach and remained open. She slipped through, into another tunnel, and followed until she had no idea of how far they had gone. This tunnel leveled out, and there were many doors. After a while she was walking on bare earth, then on stone.

The tunnel curved downward again, so steeply that steps were cut into the stone. She stumbled once, her feet so numb she could hardly feel them, but caught herself on the wall and hung there, gasping, desperately afraid that her father had heard her. But he continued on.

A while later an oozing stream crossed the tunnel, and she waded ankle-deep in frigid mud.

They seemed to go on for endless miles. Her legs were getting numb now, seeming to be leaden weights below the knees. She struggled to remain upright. Every breath was freezing torture.

At last a final door opened and the tunnel ended. Still holding the candle aloft, her father paused by the bank of an underground river which flowed through a vast cavern, out of and back into the infinite and impenetrable. The place was dimly lit by glowing blue stones set in the walls, forming a semi-circle between the tunnel mouth and the river. When Evnos extinguished the candle, the stones seemed to glow brighter.

Amadel looked up and saw huge fangs, the solid drippings of the cavern hanging in the semi-darkness. Others rose from the floor.

The glowing stones cast their long shadows. It seemed she was in the mouth of a dragon. She had been swallowed, and emotion came back to her in a sudden rush of awakening, a kind of unreasoning, helpless terror. The urge to scream was almost unbearable. She bit her fist hard to keep herself silent.

And there was a new terror. For the first time she wondered what her father would do if he found her here. She hid among the stone teeth.

Then she saw, by the edge of the evil stream, what had to be some sort of marble structure, half a bed, half an altar. Bones lay on it, pale and thin bones, like those she had seen so often in the courtyard above. She was not afraid of mere bones, but when she saw that the skeleton was dressed in moldering rags which had once been a fine gown, and that the fingers were still laden with golden rings very much like the ones she herself owned, and that the skull wore a crown marked with the sign of the Phoenix, the emblem of her own house, she felt a strong inner terror indeed, far worse than all that had gone before.

She was out of her stupor. The sharp fear had driven away the previous numbing shock. Now she was all eyes and ears, watching, listening, trying to survive.

There was more. Evnos knelt before the altar and began to speak.

"Dearest, I have returned to you. You are the source of all my strength. You know that. My heart is heavy, heavier than it has ever been. I don't know how I shall go on. Our daughter is lost to us. She has defiled herself. She has defied me. She has cut herself off irrevocably from our house, from Iankoros, from the lineage of the princes. I can't bring her back. What shall I do? What? You always seem to know. Help me now."

He paused and leaned forward, as if listening. Then his voice rose. He broke into tears.

"Beloved, can it be that all we have struggled for has come to nothing? I was angry with her, yes, but inside I was very hurt. I died a little, at each stage of her degradation. I died when I saw her lie with him. I watched through my glass, mad with grief and shame and anger. I didn't know what to do. I wanted to send a demon to tear the two of them to bits. But I controlled myself. I drew rein on my temper. I showed mercy. I know what should be done to an impure member of the house of the princes, according to our ancient law. But I couldn't. *She is our daughter.* So I spared her life. But I felt the pain that only a father can feel, when his child is no longer his child. She even tried to cast herself from her window to escape me forever. Am I so terrible? *Does she prefer Rannon to me?*"

His sobs were hoarse and rasping, interspersed with coughing.

The cavern echoed deeply with the sound. He seemed very old and frail just then.

After a while he was silent, again listening. He nodded more than once, then whispered, "Yes, you are right. We must talk of other things." He rambled on in a disjointed manner, telling of imaginary intrigues, the economy of the kingdom, wars, the doings of ministers, of court tournaments and fêtes. It hardly made sense to Amadel. It was like an incomplete tale to her, imperfectly copied from an old book.

Evnos spoke lovingly to the dead thing. He climbed onto the marble platform and lay down beside the heap of bones. He kissed the skull. The crown slid off, clanking against stone. He put his arms around the delicate shoulders. Bones rattled inside the ruined gown, and Amadel could stand it no longer. She bit her hand again, then stuffed her sleeve into her mouth to stifle a scream, but it came anyway as a low, whining moan, and suddenly her knees folded under her. She swooned.

She lay semi-conscious for a time she could not measure, then felt hands lifting her up. After a while she could see a little. She was raised up, out of nightmare into living horror.

Evnos held her by the arms. They stood before the altar. He nodded to the bones.

"So my daughter has followed me to this secret place," he said. "So the defiled one knows everything. It is well that you should, you who are unclean, you who are no longer a princess of Iankoros." He let go of one arm and turned her head, holding her chin in his hand. "Now you know. Look. This is your mother, my beloved Riacinera."

She could only scream, "They're bones! They're just bones!"

She pounded on his chest with her free hand, then wriggled and broke free. She ran for the passageway, staggering on leaden feet, gasping for breath, clawing at the tunnel walls. She felt her way in utter darkness, along the frigid passages, through many doors, sometimes crawling on cold stone and earth, until at last she came to the door that opened into the armory.

Even the relative gloom there dazzled her, but she did not pause. She ran out into the light of day, covering her eyes, and groped again along walls, across a courtyard, in through a doorway, up the stairs to her room.

She fell down on her bed and muffled her shrieks in a pillow.

The spirits gathered around her, clucking softly like birds.

14 The Reveries

PRINCE EVNOS (in darkness):

Bones, child? I have lost you, yes, and everything, everything is bones now. All the world is bone and ash, the ruin of what once was fair. I truly remember how it was. The voices within me will not let me rest. There is a power that rises up, awesome and unseen like a bottomless sea of spirits, crying *"Hear us! Hear us!"* And I answer, *"Speak! Speak! I will hear you!"* Yet they only cry all the louder, *"Hear us! Hear us, mad one, who has slain us all!"*

When they call me mad, I know that I am. This wailing in the mind betokens madness, I am sure. My walls are breached. An invincible army presses against the fortress of my reason, presses, presses — I fear. I tremble. I can only surrender. I say to myself, "What is this? What am I to make of this?" I hide behind a mask of bewilderment, and still I die a slow death within me, a death that has been mine since first I opened my eyes into this world. Oh, that my mother's womb had been my grave, and she had died forever great with me. I curse the day on which I was born and curse him who came to my father saying that he had a son, making him very glad. Let there be no more gladness. I am weary of rejoicing. I find it merely false, like a festive mask which has lost its glitter and is now just crumpled paper and wood.

Let those who shout for joy be silent. Let those who dance be still.

Let no more children come into the world, and let midwives be slaughtered for the good of mankind. Then will the Earth be virgin again as it was before the day the gods, the conspiring, cowardly gods fled from the Plain of Leboladen and gave Rannon the victory. Let the gods themselves be cursed and silenced and stilled.

(A pause. Shutters flap in the wind. Rain pours rattling through a ruined ceiling. The Prince shivers, drawing his cloak around himself.)

My eyes are open now, and I have seen the end. I have seen the beginning too, and I know how I came to be where I now stand. Child, I wanted to teach you great magic, to reveal hidden worlds to you. I wanted you to reach out and touch the Moon in its rising and change the course of time. I think you could do that. I wanted you to follow after me, to be greater than I ever was.

But magic would have only opened your eyes that much sooner. It is better to be blind. The truth is far worse than comforting, oblivion-bringing lies. You learn a little thing at first, and this leads to another, and yet another, until knowledge becomes vast and dense and terrible, and you are overwhelmed. And in the end — terror! All is nakedly revealed. Beyond you, the abyss.

I could not give you that, my child. Let that not be my legacy to you, flesh of my flesh.

For me there is no forgiveness. I was unjust in my search for justice. In taking what was rightly mine, I became a thief. I made excuses for myself and so became inexcusable.

I shall seek no more. Theremderis would understand. You would have liked him, child. I wish you could have met more than his bones. He taught me much, everything there is except wisdom.

Teacher, hear me. I tried — tried to make some good come out of my wreck, so that the cold ashes might stir again in some dim future. There is nothing for me. In my idle fancies — yes, in my madness — Riacinera has returned. She hasn't changed. In my mind she is as young as she ever was, and her laughter and her smile have not altered.

But I have changed. I am not the same. I cannot reach out, even to her. Not anymore. And so I am alone, alone down the long track of empty years.

AMADEL (before a lantern, her face aglow with light):

When first I knew of the world beyond the island, I had a dream which frightened me. I saw a huge spider of the night, whose flesh was the darkness, whose web was the sky, from which the stars hung like drops of dew. I watched him climbing back and forth in the sky and up and down in it, regarding the Earth as a morsel he had caught but not yet eaten. He descended slowly, slowly, and his jaws gaped wide.

That was my dark dream. I have dreamed also of green fields, of palaces and cities and towns, of mountains and broad plains, of rivers thick with ships. I have seen these things in my books, and Menas spoke of them, and he came to me from those places, from those fields, those cities. My dear Menas had seen the knights in splendid armor and the maidens in their fine dresses.

When I sleep sometimes, I see them still, and when I wake I look out of my prison over hills of gray mud furrowed by the rain. For much of my life I thought this island the whole world, and my father the one, the primal man, all-powerful like a god.

Truly dreams are to be preferred, for waking is cruel; but I have awakened.

Now I have seen the night spider again and he has my father's face. His house is the house of Death, strewn with bones, and my father has invited Death to come and dwell in Iankoros, crouching invisible among the bones. I think this land was green once, before Death came, but I know it will never be green again.

Menas! Sweet, dear, beloved Menas, please don't think me a traitor if some hero comes to me and I go with him. I shall owe him that much. Somehow I shall call such a hero to me, out of the cities and towns, out of the green fields, across the seas, as Halymon did when she was held by the giant, or as Nalea did on Dregmond's mountain. It shall be my great task, to summon him, and for this alone I endure my days.

15 The Coming of the Hero

AMADEL RARELY GAZED from her window anymore. The bedroom was too confining, too oppressive. She spent much of her time in the open, on a porch high among the rooftops of the castle. When the weather was fair, she slept there too. She sat for months as the seasons changed, no longer weeping. Often she sang to herself, halfway hoping that somehow her somber songs would drift over the sea on the wind, and reach the ears of a knight who would come and rescue her. But still the days crept slowly past, and the rain and snow came, and she retreated inside.

That winter was the most dismal she had ever known. The castle remained dark, cold, and empty. She never saw her father, and did not want to see him. She fled from the sound of his approach, and took to dining in the great hall at strange hours so as to deliberately avoid him.

He spent the nights, and the days too, in his tower reading from his books and chanting mysterious names.

With the return of spring, the birds came to Amadel. They gathered around her by the hundreds on the porch, and said to her, "Why is the lady sad, who spoke to us and gave us food? Are there not sun and wind and food?"

"I have no wings," she replied. "Therefore I am sad. But I don't think it will do any good to weep. I am sad because I cannot fly away from this place as you do."

"You're too heavy to carry."

These words called into her mind something she had read long ago, something quite common in the romances. She bade a gull come a little closer, spreading crumbs in her lap. As the bird ate, she tore a scrap from the margin of a book, and wrote on it a plea to some unknown hero, telling of her woes and her predicament. She took the bird in her hand and tied the message to its leg with a strand of her hair, then set the bird free.

After that she wrote a message a day and sent it with a bird, and in time she counted a hundred birds, and it was midsummer. She knew some of the notes would be lost in the sea, some rubbed off on the rocks of the Black Cliffs, and a few puzzled over by the man who dumped fish guts on the wharf in Nedek. But one or two might meet other eyes. Still she hoped, and stole parchment from her father to write more messages.

She wished desperately for something to happen, for there to be an end.

One morning in early autumn she woke from a troubled sleep on the hard stones of the porch where she had rolled from a straw mattress laid close by, and found the air filled with flapping birds. They swarmed over her and perched on the roofs, on ledges, on chairs. She waved drifting feathers away from her face.

"What has happened? Friends, why do you come like this?"

"A ship! It's a ship!"

"Where?"

"Look! Look!"

From where she sat, she had a wide view of the island and the sea.

The ship was there, rising and falling gently in the waves, its sails white and filled with wind, a scarlet emblem across the broad mainsail. Banners writhed from the mast like long serpents. Amadel could barely make out the men on the decks, dozens of them, more people than she had ever imagined could be on such a vessel. It was as if half the world were coming to her.

The ship passed out of sight beneath the cliffs, steering, she knew, for the island's harbor.

She thanked the birds and hurried away. She ran to her room and looked at herself in the mirror. The face she saw was nothing out of any romance, dirty, with matted, stringy hair. Her gown had been white once; now it was gray and brown, trailing tatters. She was barefoot, her feet almost black.

It was simple: the hero had come for a *princess* to take to his own land, and he would find a princess, not a beggar girl.

She washed herself in a tub that was filled from a cistern of rainwater on the roof. Then she put on her finest gown, flowing blue with gems set in it like stars in the night sky. Her hair was still a wet tangle, so she dried it as best she could, then pinned it up and put on her golden tiara, in which was set the emblem of the Phoenix, carven in an oval of ivory. Last, she slipped her feet gingerly into leather shoes patterned with golden scales.

When all was ready, she descended to the main courtyard of the castle. There she stood stiffly, waiting, gazing up at the empty towers and crumbling rooftops. Before her was the gate. She went over to the mechanism and tried to lower the drawbridge, but the great levers and gears would not turn. The portcullis would not rise.

"Defiled One, you have forgotten the charm I laid on this place. Never shall any gate open for you, as long as I live."

She whirled about in suddenly remembered horror and beheld her father. She hardly recognized him: shockingly aged, his shoulders stooped, his hair and beard almost entirely gray, his face drawn and lined, his eyes sunken and read. He wore armor that hardly fit him. Pulled on hastily over his customary garb was a finely-wrought breastplate with the sign of the Phoenix outlined in rubies. His arm and leg guards, his mail and helmet were silver. The great sword Dran hung at his side. He bore a black, featureless, triangular shield.

"Father, why are you here?"

"To repel the invader. To drive off this pirate who comes to seize what is not his."

As he spoke, metal-shod feet tramped up to the gate. There were perhaps a dozen men outside the castle. They stopped suddenly, and a voice called out, "How now, wizard? Where is this maiden you hold captive?"

Prince Evnos all but spat his reply. "Go away, little boy, before I punish you. My sword has a powerful doom on it, and no man can conquer me."

Evnos drew out Dran and waved the gleaming blade in the air. He began to shout with the greatest confidence, but then his voice faltered, and he ended in despair.

"The doom is this, put on the sword Dran by the King of the Dwarves: Many heads shall this sword cut off . . . but the *last* shall be . . . the head . . . of wisdom."

Amadel heard him whisper to himself, "And after wisdom? The power is fled. Theremderis, forgive me. I understand now. My ending is just." He began to weep.

"What is the matter?" called the voice from beyond the gate. "Lost your tongue, coward?"

Metal clanged. A grappling hook caught on the battlement above the raised drawbridge.

Evnos turned to Amadel and spoke softly.

131

"Daughter, I must fight as a warrior now, not as a wizard. When I was young I took an oath. I swore on Dran to protect this island, and the magic of Dran is spent. It is merely a sword now, powered only by the strength of my arm. I am going to die, and it is your doing. I do not forgive you for what you have done, nor should you forgive me. We are past all forgiveness, both of us. We do what we must . . . then merely go our separate ways. But I shall not depart into the lands of Rannon. I have found a way to escape him. It is a secret discovered by the greatest and cleverest of wizards, long ago. He blew his soul out like a candle's flame even before he died. He lived, his mind aware, his body moving for a time, but he had no soul. When he died, there was only dust. My faithless, worthless daughter, you have brought me to dust. No one will mourn for me, not even you. Now I must sing my own dirge. I only ask that you listen in silence. Do me this last honor. If you can, try to remember some of the words. I require nothing more of you."

"But, Father, why do you have to die at all?" Suddenly she pitied him. The realization was so startling it frightened her. "You said yourself that I was worthless, a thing without value to you. Please, just take your spell off the gate and let me go. Why should you die for one who is defiled?"

"*Silence!* Can you not obey me *even now?*" There was much pain in his voice, in his eyes, Amadel thought, and much confusion. Her father was like one sleepwalking, acting out a dream. He began to sing his own funeral dirge, in a fine, deep voice, with dignity and grace, as befitted one of his ancient lineage.

"I am Thindarek's son, so great a hero,
And to his ghost I sing, this solemn death-song.
Of old I swore my oath; it is not broken.
With Dran in hand I stand, and face the foeman."

The verses went on and on, telling of his deeds, all his strivings, his hopes, his failures, his guilt and sorrow. The tale of the bride Riacinera was told in full, and Amadel listened intently. Suddenly she appreciated how magnificent a man he had been, how his life had been a foolish, terrible irony, and his death would be even more terrible if he died here, now, for the sake of some ancient oath and a daughter whose name he would not speak.

"Father! Stop! Don't die! I'll send him away and stay with you forever! *Listen to me!*"

He looked at her sadly, but continued. He finished his last verse:

"And far from Rannon's land, I have rescued her.
Far down beneath the earth, her soul is ashes.

132

Now for his bonded slave, he shall not have her.
Now as my last night comes, I die contented."

By this time the foreign knight was on top of the wall. He turned back to his followers, raised his sword, and they cheered. Then he lowered his rope into the courtyard and slid down.

Amadel saw him clearly for the first time: tall, muscular, his hair sun-bleached and his face brown. He wore copper-plated armor, with the red sign of a serpent and a fish emblazoned on his surcoat and shield. He, like her father, carried a long sword.

He dropped to the pavement with a clatter, staggering for an instant, then recovering, and seemed about to speak another challenge, but the words never came.

"So you are the one," said Prince Evnos calmly.

The knight's sudden awe was gone. "Yes, I am the one. Now meet your death on the edge of an honest sword. I spit at your magic and your dooms."

"Let us fight then," Evnos said.

Amadel stood to one side, weeping.

They fought, and sparks flew where Dran bit into the other blade, or smote the foreign knight's shield. Throughout the day the two men contended, and poets have since made much of that combat, telling again and again of the wizard and the warrior in that courtyard, how sometimes Prince Evnos seemed almost about to win, with the knight at his mercy; then again how the knight sprang up with renewed strength.

The sun crossed the sky. Both of them battled on in the shifting shadows, bleeding from terrible wounds, their swords notched like saws, their armor and shields tarnished and dented. Both stood amazed at the skill and endurance of the other, and at times, as they paused to rest, they complimented one another and did each other honor, as if they were old comrades in arms, lifelong friends. All the while the only witnesses were the girl Amadel, the skull of Theremderis, which still lay where it had fallen so many years before, and the empty windows.

There seemed to be magic in Dran yet, a magical strength which kept Evnos going when he should have fallen down exhausted. The knight came to realize as he caught the blows of his increasingly shapeless shield, as sweat streamed over his eyes and his heart pounded, that this old man would surely be the victor unless he somehow lost hold of that sword.

So the knight took a new strategy, and only feinted when he seemed to seek the Prince's throat and breast.

"I've got you!" gasped Evnos. "You fight less fiercely now!"

Then the knight struck a blow with all his might, not at the Prince's vitals, but at his wrist. It caught Evnos by surprise and connected, slicing through with little resistance. The knight reeled with the unspent force of the stroke, while Evnos cried out, holding his spouting stump.

Dran, and the hand that still held it, dropped spinning to the pavement.

Desperately, in what he knew was to be his last breath, the Prince recited a short formula he had arrived at after many years of labor and seclusion. It was the final secret of Hinaris, that greatest of wizards, who alone of all men had managed to escape Rannon.

He spoke the words. It was done. He was safe now, his soul extinguished from his body. When the last word was spoken, he smiled and turned to his daughter.

She was his living emblem of defiance. He had snatched her out of Rannon's grasp. "I have won," he said aloud. "Don't you see? I have fooled the pig-head for the last time. Let him howl. Let the Earth shake. I have won. Perhaps, in the future, someone will free all the souls in the Underearth and defeat him utterly —"

Then the knight, coming up from behind, brought his sword down hard on the Prince's helmet, crashing down through the skull almost to the jawbone.

The body collapsed. The knight drew his sword from the ruined head. Blood poured out of the battered helmet, pooling on the stones.

The knight fell to his knees, too exhausted to rise. He looked up at Amadel, who stood amazed.

"What did he mean? What was he talking about?"

"I don't know," she said. "I think he had gone mad with grief."

She began to weep.

Much later, the gate was opened, the portcullis raised, the drawbridge eased gently down; and so the knight emerged, leading the princess by the hand. Soldiers whom he had commanded to await him there let out a great shout of victory. The knight could only manage a weak smile and Amadel a sigh.

The ship waited for them in the harbor. Again, more men cheered. Trumpets blew. The knight stood at the end of the gangplank, waiting for Amadel to precede him.

"Lady," he said. "Will you come with me now, away from this place?"

"Yes," she replied, as if completing some long-rehearsed ritual. "I have lived here too long. I want to see the world now."

This is the ending of the tale of Prince Evnos and Lady Riacinera, of Amadel and Menas, and the house and the princes of Iankoros. There were no more princes.

Emanath was the knight's name, and in later years he was called "The Great." He took his lady away from the dead isle, and she gazed only ahead as they voyaged, never back, as the ship bore them over the sea to his own country. There she lived with him all the days of her life. She took the name Lamilim Yin, which means "child of sea and air," and she bore him four sons, who were children of the earth. Of this knight Emanath, his lady Lamilim Yin, and their sons, the tales are many and long, but there is no room for them here.

Appendix:

The Vision of Morosa Etewah

. . . Before the beginning of the world, there was only Morosa Etewah, whose name may be read but never spoken, sitting supreme and complete in the void of Unbeing. Both male and female was This One, encompassing all principles, all thoughts.

A vision came to Morosa Etewah, revealing that which might one day arise out of the Unbeing. Before anything was created, This One viewed all things, even unto the End, when living and unliving alike shall return to the mind of Morosa Etewah, like a forest of trees shrinking backwards into a single seed.

And much that Morosa Etewah saw was pleasing, and much unpleasing, but This One willed a beginning, that the vision of Morosa Etewah should follow its appointed course.

Therefore This One raised a hand, causing there to be time and duration, that the vision might remain.

Then Morosa Etewah dreamed a mighty dream, remembering the primal vision.

Soon there stood in the darkness the Nargotri, the whispering thoughts of Morosa Etewah, called only the Nargotri as This One dreamed them. Later, men took them to be gods and called them by many individual names, but Morosa Etewah beheld them and dreamed them only as beacons standing against the darkness, and needed no further distinction.

Now these Nargotri were lesser than Morosa Etewah, for they

could not share in the wholeness of This One. They discovered themselves to be potent only in pairs, so they shaped themselves male and female, each of them half the image of Morosa Etewah.

The dream continued, as yet untroubled by the strangeness of the Nargotri. Morosa Etewah called on his Thoughts to dream also, to recapture the fleeting instant of the first vision, in which there had been not merely duration, but place.

So they dreamed together, This One above all, and the Nargotri, male and female as they had shaped themselves.

And the Earth was, lifeless and flat like a plate, tumbling over and over in the darkness of Unbeing. So it remained for an eon, or for the blinking of the eye. All time is one for Morosa Etewah, whose upraised hand caused the beginning of time.

Now This One regarded the Nargotri, the halflings, male and female, seeking to make them whole. This One seized a pair them, in the right hand and in the left, and pressed the two Nargotri together, as a potter presses clay, that they might be joined in the true image of Morosa Etewah.

But the Nargotri merely lost their forms in the hands of Morosa Etewah, until no semblance of them remained. This is a great mystery. The wise do not agree on its meaning. Some say that the two Nargotri had rebelled, others that there are laws binding even This One, from a source greater even than the vision of Morosa Etewah (and let men ask, *whence came the vision?*), forbidding the union.

The shapes which had been Nargotri burned fiercely in the hands of This One, until all their substance was consumed, and only light remained. Then Morosa Etewah, in sadness, released them into the Unbeing, where they still remain. Men call them Sun and Moon. They are still male and female. The stars are their children.

Among the surviving Nargotri was that creature later called Rannon, male in shape, who recoiled in terror and rage from the hands of Morosa Etewah. He withdrew from the company of the others, far into the void of Unbeing, and there brooded for more time than can be counted. Slowly his terror diminished, but his rage waxed greater, and he swore vengeance against Morosa Etewah, not because he mourned those Nargotri who were the first of all created things to die, but to remove any possible threat to himself.

Evil was born then.

Rannon is called the Untrue Nargotri.

Meanwhile Morosa Etewah steadied the tumbling Earth with a hand, setting it afloat on the Unbeing as delicately as a child places a leaf on the surface of a still pool. This One and all the remaining True Nargotri looked on the world, and dreamed of it again, giving shape to the lands, raising the mountains, driving the waters down from the hills and off the plains, into their proper beds.

But the shape of the lands would not remain, and the waters poured down into the abyss.

So Morosa Etewah alone created the first thing of flesh, the serpent Shōmar, and commanded Shōmar to wind himself around the rim of the world, so that the waters should remain.

But Shōmar was too short, and still the waters poured over the edge, through the gap between his head and tail. Therefore Morosa Etewah placed golden rings on the tail of the serpent. Their glitter caught Shōmar's eye, and at once he sought them, but even as he did, the gold moved further away. Thus Shōmar continues to chase his tail, and shall pursue it without rest until the end of time, and by his motion all things remain on the surface of the Earth.

For the heart of Shōmar beats fiercely like a drum, and the scales of Shōmar are hot as molten iron. When the oceans fall on the back of Shōmar there is a great thundering, and steam rises, becoming clouds, which drift over the world, returning the waters to the waters, as Morosa Etewah dreamed the rivers and the lakes and the great ocean. Thus the circle of being is laid out for men to see, even as trees grow from small seeds, only to produce seeds again.

Shōmar likewise brings the seasons. There are four elements from which the world is made, arranged into four zones, each blending into the next where they meet. In the middle, where the four are joined, are the lands of men.

The first element is ice, to absorb the heat of the serpent. Ice lies to the north of the world. To the east is water, to the south air, to the west fire. When the head of the serpent is in the north, Shōmar breathes winter over the lands. For all that his hide may be molten, when his breath howls through the mountain passes, it drives the blizzard before it. These things Morosa Etewah and the True Nargotri have dreamed.

When the serpent reaches the place where the ice melts, his breath becomes watery spray, and the spring rains come. To the east the oceans have no end, pouring directly onto Shōmar.

To the south is the Great Stone Waste, and beyond that, empty air. When Shōmar breathes the warm air of summer, grain ripens. Then he moves to the west, into the dying fire of the sunset, which touches winter's ice, the autumn comes, leaves turning red and gold and finally brittle brown with the touch of those strangely cool flames, and with the passage of Shōmar.

Thus the world assumed its present shape. The elements mixed like swirling paints in the dreams of Morosa Etewah, and more living creatures rose out of the Unbeing, to crawl and walk upon the earth, to swim in the seas, to fly in the skies. Male and female were conjoined, bringing forth life of innumerable kinds, each portioned out of air and earth and ice after their kind.

Mankind is made of fire and earth, like all the beasts of the land, who can neither swim beneath the sea nor rise upon the air.

Ice is found only in evil creatures, in the hostile things of the night, and perhaps too in the most evil of men, who set themselves apart in forbidden places.

Of the icy lands to the north, little is known, for only the dead set their course thither.

But death itself only came into the world when the Untrue Nargotri, called Rannon, returned from his sojourn in the depths of Unbeing. He made war on the others, on all created things, and those journeys to the ice lands began.

Then the dreams of Morosa Etewah were dark.

www.ingramcontent.com/pod-product-compliance
Lightning Source LLC
Chambersburg PA
CBHW050757250626
47155CB00005B/2105